VALENTINE CROW
and Mr. Death

VALENTINE CROW
and Mr. Death

Jenni Spangler

SIMON & SCHUSTER

First published in Great Britain in 2023 by Simon & Schuster UK Ltd

Text and illustrations copyright © 2023 Jenni Spangler

1 3 5 7 9 10 8 6 4 2

Simon & Schuster UK Ltd
1st Floor, 222 Gray's Inn Road, London
WC1X 8HB

www.simonandschuster.co.uk
www.simonandschuster.com.au
www.simonandschuster.co.in

Simon & Schuster Australia, Sydney
Simon & Schuster India, New Delhi

A CIP catalogue record for this book is available from the British Library.

PB ISBN 978-1-3985-0466-0
eBook ISBN 978-1-3985-0467-7
eAudio ISBN 978-1-3985-0468-4

Typeset in the UK
Printed and Bound in the UK using 100% Renewable Electricity
at CPI Group (UK) Ltd

MIX
Paper | Supporting
responsible forestry
FSC® C171272

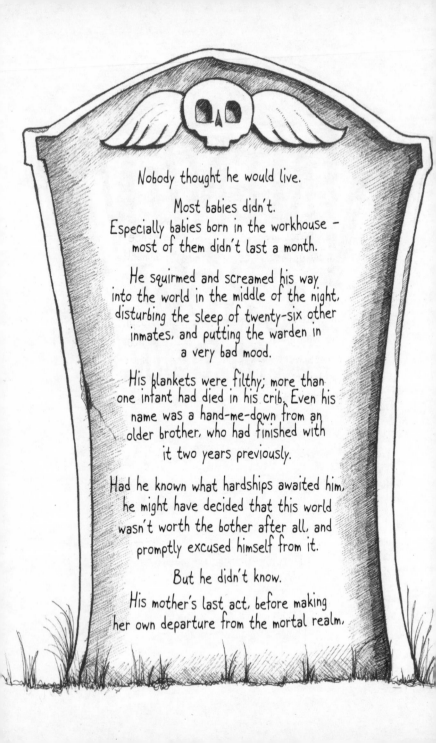

Nobody thought he would live.

Most babies didn't.
Especially babies born in the workhouse —
most of them didn't last a month.

He squirmed and screamed his way
into the world in the middle of the night,
disturbing the sleep of twenty-six other
inmates, and putting the warden in
a very bad mood.

His blankets were filthy; more than
one infant had died in his crib. Even his
name was a hand-me-down from an
older brother, who had finished with
it two years previously.

Had he known what hardships awaited him,
he might have decided that this world
wasn't worth the bother after all, and
promptly excused himself from it.

But he didn't know.

His mother's last act, before making
her own departure from the mortal realm,

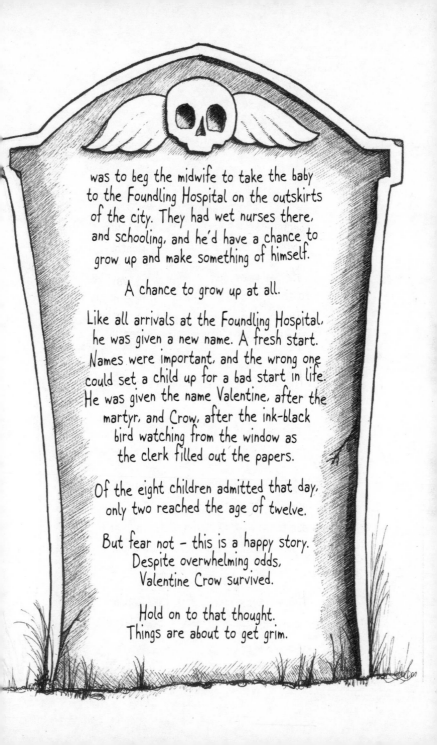

was to beg the midwife to take the baby to the Foundling Hospital on the outskirts of the city. They had wet nurses there, and schooling, and he'd have a chance to grow up and make something of himself.

A chance to grow up at all.

Like all arrivals at the Foundling Hospital, he was given a new name. A fresh start. Names were important, and the wrong one could set a child up for a bad start in life. He was given the name Valentine, after the martyr, and Crow, after the ink-black bird watching from the window as the clerk filled out the papers.

Of the eight children admitted that day, only two reached the age of twelve.

But fear not - this is a happy story. Despite overwhelming odds, Valentine Crow survived.

Hold on to that thought. Things are about to get grim.

Perchance to Dream

L ike all the best stories, Valentine's began with
an ending.

On the most important day of his life so far, he
woke before the morning bell. He sprang from his bed and
dressed in his first ever set of brand-new clothes, folded his
old Foundling uniform neatly and combed his hair.

He lined up for breakfast, said his prayers and ate his porridge
in silence, just as he had done every morning for as long as he
could remember. But today everything seemed different. Today,
his time as a Foundling was over. He was to head out through
the big iron gates and into the wide world as an apprentice.
The dining room felt smaller than it had the night before.
Time moved far too slowly – after nearly twelve years of waiting,
Valentine couldn't bear to wait a single second longer.

Nine boys and eleven girls were leaving the hospital that day. They had been prepared for this moment since they were tiny children, by learning to read and write and dig and sew, to follow orders and mind their manners and remember their place.

Single file, they marched across the courtyard to the main reception building, every one of them extremely grown-up. Dozens of little faces appeared at the windows as the smaller children watched and waved goodbye before being ushered off to their schoolrooms.

They were seated on low benches along the corridor, beneath the grand oil paintings of the hospital's most important donors. The first three boys were called into the bursar's office to meet their masters, the keepers of

their new adventures. A large clock sternly counted out their remaining seconds before everything would change. A girl was summoned in, then ten minutes later, two more.

Eventually only two children were left – Valentine Crow and Philomena Sparrow. They had arrived at the hospital on the same day, and they were to leave on the same day also.

'Where do you think you'll be sent?' asked Philomena, leaning across the gap

2

between their benches.

Out of sheer habit, Valentine glanced up and down the corridor to make sure they were alone. Boys and girls weren't supposed to mix in the Foundling Hospital and talking in the corridors was also strictly forbidden.

'You can't get in trouble for talking to me now,' said Philomena, before he had the chance to reply. 'We're not Foundlings any more! Freedom at last!'

'I know! The school master says a lot of us will be going off to sea. He says the ocean's so big you can go for weeks without ever seeing land. Nothing but water to the edges of the earth,' Valentine said excitedly. Dangerous work, sailing, but a man could make his fortune if he was stubborn enough to survive.

'Is that what you want to do?'

'Not sure.'

His stomach was tingly with excitement and nerves. It was as though there were two people inside him, fighting for control. The fearless, grown-up adventurer who was ready to sample everything the world had to offer, and the orphan who'd spent all of his short life within the hospital walls and didn't know how he'd ever get by outside them. But he knew that his master would be his ticket out of here.

Philomena must be feeling it too because he'd never seen her so fidgety.

'You're lucky,' she said. 'I'll be in service, no doubt, cleaning out someone else's chamber pots for the rest of my life—'

'—And be grateful for it,' they finished in unison, and both laughed. If there was one ultimate lesson the Foundlings were taught, it was to be grateful to their elders and betters. They were poor little outcasts, and everything they had was the result of the generosity of others. Foundlings were frequently reminded that cheerful obedience and honest labour were the route to happiness, and if that meant cleaning out chamber pots for a living, then so be it.

'What would you pick, if you could do anything?' Philomena asked.

A difficult question. The world lay spread out before him like a feast, to pick and choose from all its delights. 'I could be happy as a gardener, I reckon. Watching things grow. Or on a farm. Looking after the animals.'

'Do you remember the lamb Missus Price raised by hand? Used to follow her about like a puppy?'

'Oh! That's right!' The memory, as warm and fuzzy as lambswool, popped back into his mind. For their first few years, Valentine and Philomena had been fostered in the countryside. He couldn't remember much from when he was tiny, but he knew they'd had the freedom of the farmyard and outbuildings, running barefoot through the mud and grass. Until they were five years old and reclaimed by the Foundling Hospital, thrust into a world of uniforms and straight lines and strict rules.

It had been a sudden and bewildering change and Valentine didn't care to think about it. Better to think of the future, instead – of the exciting possibilities ahead.

'Or I could be . . .' Valentine scrabbled to change the subject. 'I know – a baker. I could stuff myself with pies and cakes and never eat porridge again.'

'Good riddance to porridge!' said Philomena. 'I want a proper adventure. Somewhere there's no walls and no rules. Nobody telling me what to do every second of the day. In fact –' she stretched her feet out and tipped her head back – 'I'd be happy just to have my own door.'

'A door?'

'Right. Then I can open it or close it and decide whether to let anyone inside. Not have to listen to twenty girls snoring all night long.'

'All by yourself?' said Valentine. 'Wouldn't you be lonely?'

'I might let you come and visit, if you bring some of those pies.' She smiled and peered at him from the corner of her eye. 'So long as you never tell me what to do.'

'I promise,' said Valentine. It all sounded perfect, except that they were about to be separated and sent off to who-knows-where for seven years. He leaned towards her urgently. 'How will we find each other again?'

Before she could reply, the door to the bursar's office opened and they both snapped upright, eyes forward, hands in their laps. They might not be under Foundling rules any more, but years of training had left their mark.

'Miss Sparrow, come this way, please.'

She stood and followed the bursar, giving Valentine one last nod as she disappeared through the door.

And then he was alone.

No one was ever alone at the Foundling Hospital. They ate together, played together, worked together – even slept two to a bed. It was much too quiet now. What was taking so long? It was afternoon, according to the stern clock. The rest of the Foundlings would be sweeping the floor and tidying away the benches after dinner, ready for their afternoon tasks. Had he been forgotten? If his master didn't come, would he have to put his uniform back on, and return to the schoolroom? He couldn't bear it, not now he'd come this close to escape. The world outside was calling to him.

At long last, the bursar's door opened once more.

'Come in, Valentine Crow. Your master won't be much longer now. You can wait in my office.'

Sunlight streamed in through the tall windows and specks of dust swam and danced within it. It was peaceful, and despite his eagerness to be out in the world, Valentine knew he would miss this place.

The bursar unrolled a scroll of parchment and handed Valentine a quill. 'Your apprenticeship papers. Sign here.'

The sheet was covered with dense

writing in a thick, looping hand. Valentine's fingers hovered above the page as he tried to skim it quickly and figure out which trade he was entering.

'A very good prospect . . . No shortage of work! I daresay I'll patronize your business myself, one of these days.' The bursar tapped the line for Valentine's signature. 'Write your name, here.'

He did as he was told, and the document was whisked away and tightly re-rolled.

'Who will—' Valentine began, but he was interrupted by three heavy knocks on the grand front door.

'This will be him,' said the bursar, slipping through a second doorway towards the main entry. 'He's a little late, but no matter.'

'Normally,' a gravelly, unfamiliar voice replied, 'people complain that I'm early.'

'Aaaargh!' the bursar cried out. There was a thud and a smash as something heavy was knocked over. 'Saints preserve us!'

Valentine darted across the floor and peered round the half-open door, alarmed and curious.

'I'm here to collect my apprentice,' said the stranger's voice.

'There's been a mistake.' The bursar was leaning against the wall, one hand clutching the edge of a table for support, the

shattered remains of a vase at his feet.

Whoever he was talking to was hidden from Valentine's view, but the bursar looked terrified.

For a moment, Valentine wondered whether staying at the hospital would be so bad after all, if it meant never meeting the owner of that unnerving voice.

But only for a moment. He made a decision to be brave and face his future head on.

'Where is the child?'

No use delaying it. Valentine took a deep breath and stepped through the door.

'Here I am.'

The man, no, the *thing*, turned its skull towards Valentine and regarded him with two soot-black holes where his eyes should have been.

It was person-shaped, but definitely not a person. It was extremely tall, head scraping the ceiling. Where the face should have been was only bone, and it was clothed in a long, ragged gown, which wasn't black, exactly, but some darker colour which didn't have a name.

'Valentine Crow,' said the creature, stretching out long, sinewy fingers towards him in greeting. Although its mouth was simply two rows of bare teeth and no lips, Valentine somehow knew it was smiling. 'Pleased to make your acquaintance. I'm Death.'

Met His Maker

V alentine put out a trembling arm and shook hands with Death. 'How do you do?'

Impossibly long and bony fingers enclosed Valentine's small hand. They were dry and smooth and clicked together like a bundle of twigs.

'This can't . . . You mustn't . . .' the bursar groaned, swaying unsteadily.

'Don't act surprised. It's hardly my first visit to this place.' Death let go of Valentine's hand and ran a finger across the top of a picture frame, wiping the dust on his cloak. 'You've redecorated.'

'You can't be here for young Valentine,' the bursar protested. 'He's perfectly healthy!'

'I'm here to take him as an apprentice, as you arranged,' replied Death.

'I would never do such a thing!'

'But you did.' He deftly snatched the apprenticeship papers and unrolled them. '*This indenture . . . Hereby and forthwith . . .* et cetera, et cetera . . . Aha!' He flicked the paper. 'Read this out loud please, Valentine, from here.'

Valentine swallowed hard and stepped closer to Death. He smelled like damp cloth and warm summer soil, nutmeg and the smoke of a candle just blown out. The creature bent down almost double to hold the paper in front of Valentine's face.

'*Valentine Crow, with the con—* Um . . .' The fancy looping letters were harder to read than the plain letters they had practised in the schoolroom.

'Consent,' prompted Death. 'It means agreement, or permission.'

'*With the consent of the hospital governors, doth put himself apprentice to Mister Death . . .*'

'Dearth!' the bursar spluttered. 'With an R. It's supposed to say Mister Dearth, the watchmaker!'

'Keep going,' said Death.

'*To learn his art and serve after the manner of an apprentice for seven years.*' Valentine gazed up at the towering figure of Death. Seven years? Learn his art?

'There you have it.'

'A spelling mistake! That's all! We would never apprentice a child to you!' exclaimed the bursar.

'Ah, but you did. Jolly good idea, too. Very busy century. Lots to do.' He held the document out towards the bursar. 'This is your signature, is it not?'

'Yes, but . . .'

'And this is Master Crow's signature, and . . .' He snapped his fingers at Valentine, and pointed towards his hand.

The quill Valentine was holding was now bent and crumpled from gripping it too tightly. A smudge of ink stained his palm.

'Not to worry,' said Death. He reached a long arm down the back of his own neck as if scratching an itch and drew a long black feather out from beneath his cloak. 'Always carry my own. Ink, please?'

Valentine fetched the inkwell obediently.

Death scrawled his signature in large, unreadable letters. 'And there's mine. All official.'

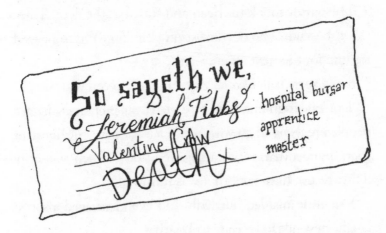

So sayeth we,
Jeremiah Tibbs — hospital bursar
Valentine Crow — apprentice
Death — master

APPRENTICE

app-REN-tiss
A person who works for little or
no pay, in order to learn a
skilled trade, such as
carpentry, shoe-making
or soul reaping.

The bursar shook his head and stared at the floor. 'I'm so sorry,' he said. 'The documents are binding. You must work for him for the next seven years.'

Seven years with Death. Valentine felt frozen with shock.

'Don't be frightened. I'm sure we'll be good friends. In fact, people are *dying* to go with me!' Death threw out his arms, then dropped them into a dejected slouch when Valentine didn't react. 'Come on, that was funny. No?'

Valentine nodded hurriedly and even managed a sort-of laugh. Best not to be rude to Death.

'We'll be on our way, then.' Death crossed to the main door and held it open for Valentine. There was no choice but to follow.

'Goodbye, Valentine Crow,' the bursar mumbled.

'Don't be glum,' said Death. 'We'll be back. See you on the . . .' He retrieved a golden watch from the folds of his cloak, opened two covers and tapped thoughtfully on the glass dial. 'Twenty-first. Take care.'

The bursar turned a funny shade of grey and swooned, landing on the stone tiles with a meaty thud.

'He's fine, only a faint,' said Death, steering Valentine through the doorway with a bony hand on his back. 'Off we go.'

They stepped on to the street and the door swung closed with a heavy, final-sounding clunk. It was a bright, clear afternoon and Valentine was shocked by how ordinary everything looked as he stood beside the spectre of Death.

With a gust of cool air, and a sound like a blanket being shaken out, Death unfurled two great feathery wings, each one as long as Valentine was tall. He gave a satisfied sigh and cracked his neck. 'Much better. This way.'

'Is the bursar really going to die on the twenty-first?' Valentine was already jogging to keep up with Death's long strides.

'No, just my little joke.' He swept round the corner and Valentine had to hop to avoid tripping over his cloak.

13

'That's unkind.'

'Nonsense,' said Death. 'Think how happy he'll be on the twenty-second!'

They reached a crossroads and Valentine stopped. This was it. This was the world. London. Though they were less than a minute's walk from the hospital, he had never been here before. There was so much life.

Brick buildings, stained black from coal soot, pressed and leaned and crowded against each other. Not neat and orderly like the buildings at the hospital – this whole placed looked like it had happened by accident, houses springing up like weeds between the paving stones, windows peeking out from under sagging roofs, washing lines strung haphazardly across alleyways, and people. So many people.

All about them, Londoners went about their business as if this was a completely normal day. They continued beating dust from rugs, climbing into carriages and carrying buckets of water. Now that he had a regular suit instead of his Foundling uniform, he could pass for one of them, but was an impostor. His nostrils stung with the odour of old fish and horse muck and burning rubbish.

'Keep up!' called Death from twenty feet ahead, and Valentine hurried to catch him.

Even more astonishing, not a single person reacted to Death as he strode amongst them.

'Do they not see you?'

'Humans are good at ignoring death. They have to be, or they'd never get anything done.' He paused and looked Valentine up and down. 'This will take for ever with your little legs.'

Death put two fingers between his teeth and whistled.

'Why—' Valentine began.

'Wait for it.'

In the far distance, thunder rumbled. Gradually the noise grew louder – not a rumble, but a steady, fast, frantic beating that grew louder and louder until it shook the pavement they were standing on. A vast, pale shape came into view and as it drew closer, Valentine saw that it was an enormous grey horse, racing towards them at an unearthly speed.

Valentine jumped backwards, certain it would trample them. But it came to a halt in front of Death, rearing up on its back legs, head level with the upstairs windows of the buildings opposite. Hoofs the size of dinner plates clattered down on to the cobbles. Across the road, two women chatting in a doorway glanced in their direction, then turned back to their conversation.

'Good boy.' Death patted the creature's neck. 'Who's a good boy?'

The beast snorted in reply. It was like no horse Valentine had ever encountered. He could see every rib and sinew through the skin as though the creature had been starved, yet it was powerful and steady. It turned its great head towards

Valentine curiously. Instead of the usual black, its eyes glowed like white-hot coals in a fireplace.

'Gytrash, this is Valentine. Our new apprentice.'

The horse snorted and stamped, shaking his long mane, which reached almost to the ground.

'Now, don't be grumpy.'

Gytrash whinnied.

'I'm sure if you give him a chance, he'll grow on you.' Death mounted the horse in a single, agile leap. 'Quick collection to do on the way home. Come on up, boy.'

Valentine looked blankly at his new master. He had never ridden a horse, let alone one as tall and terrifying as Gytrash. Death may as well have told him to grow wings and fly up there.

'Oh,' said Death. 'I see.'

Death's grip closed round Valentine's wrist, and he was yanked off his feet with tremendous strength. He scrambled to swing his leg over the horse's back. Greasy feathers, more prickly than they appeared, brushed against him as he sat behind Death on the monstrous steed.

'Hold tight. Gytrash – onwards!'

Breathed His Last

Valentine barely had time to grab Death's cloak before Gytrash reared up, then set off at a gallop through the streets.

Valentine's teeth rattled with every hoofbeat as the colossal beast raced along, squeezing between wagons without slowing, and leaping walls and fences. The world shimmered and blurred, growing dimmer and darker until they rode through swirling blackness. He clung to handfuls of fabric until his knuckles ached and he feared he would lose his grip and plunge to the ground.

Then Gytrash came to a sudden halt. Valentine was jolted forward, banging his forehead against Death's bony spine and getting a mouthful of greasy feathers.

Death leaped down effortlessly. Valentine swung his left leg

over the horse's back and
slithered down on his belly.
He landed with a thump on
the wet, cold ground
and scrambled to
his feet before those
huge hoofs could
step on him.

It seemed to
Valentine that they
were in the worst of
the city's slums. It was
as though someone had
taken the busy street
from earlier and shrunk
it down, squeezing

it into a space three sizes too small. The alleyway was barely wide enough for a dust-cart to pass through, and the crumbling houses leaned against each other as though standing upright was too exhausting. A dreadful stench of urine and coal and rot filled the air, so thick he could taste it. The sky above was so smoky, at first Valentine thought the sun had gone down.

'Good work, Gytrash.' Death took a black apple from his pocket and tossed it towards Gytrash, who caught it in his mouth and crunched and crushed it with huge yellow teeth. 'Wait for us.'

The people here were as worn out as the houses. Kids in ragged clothes ran barefoot in and out of doorways. A grey-faced woman passed them, balancing a baby on one hip and a basket on the other. Nobody looked up at the horse or the reaper. Nobody seemed surprised.

'Why are we here?' said Valentine.

'Work to do,' answered Death. 'Get used to this place. You'll visit often.' He produced the golden pocket watch and opened it – tapped it, turned a dial, rotated it in his hands.

Valentine peered through the nearest open door. A woman was grating soap into a washtub. A futile act, it seemed, because how could anyone possibly get clean in a place this dirty?

'This way.' Death shepherded him along the filthy street. They narrowly avoided a soaking from a bucket of something vile, emptied from an upstairs window. An elderly man sitting on one of the doorsteps tipped his cap to them as they passed.

'He saw us,' said Valentine, but Death didn't respond.

Near the end of the lane, they entered a tiny, dilapidated house with a bulging ceiling low enough for Valentine to touch it. Death shrank a little until he could stand without stooping. Solemnly they traced a path up the rotten, uneven stairs and found themselves in a bedroom.

Four people – three women and a vicar – were gathered beside the sickbed of a desperately thin man. The man looked right at Valentine but said nothing. No one else seemed to notice them, although the room was so small there was barely enough space for everyone in it.

Only one bed, Valentine noted. How many of these people shared it? The room was draughty, and the grate had clearly not seen a fire in a long time. These people had nothing. Nothing at all.

As a Foundling, Valentine never had anything to call his own. Not his real name, or the memory of his mother, not clothes or books or anything. Everything was shared. And yet, he now saw that he had lived in luxury compared to this. This was the poverty the hospital had rescued him from. This might've been his life, had they not taken him in.

'Are you going to . . . ?' Valentine whispered, gesturing towards the dying man.

'Very soon.' Death consulted the pocket watch again. 'His moment is almost up.'

The man coughed a horrible, deep cough and when he moved his ragged handkerchief there was blood on it. One of the women began weeping, sitting on the edge of the bed and grasping the man's hand.

'It's horrible.' Valentine wanted to cry with her. 'Why does he have to die? Why can't he stay with his family?'

'His disease has ravaged him. He's in pain. He will not get better. The sickness has brought him to the edge of life, and nothing I can do will change that. So, I extinguish the flame, and he can move on.'

'How—'

'Shhhh.' Death approached the bed, bending until his face was inches above the man's own skeletal features. 'Gideon Pike. Your hour has come, Gideon Pike.' He spoke softly, kindly, the way one might speak to a sleepy child.

Valentine expected the man to argue and beg, but he nodded.

'Did I do well?' asked the man. The others didn't seem to hear him, busy instead comforting each other. 'I tried to be a good provider.'

'You worked hard,' said Death. 'You've earned your rest.'

'Thank you,' said the man, tears threatening to spill, though he blinked them away. 'Should I close my eyes?'

'Yes,' whispered Death. His long fingers reached forward

and grasped at the air in front of the man's face. As he withdrew his hand, the faintest orange shape came with it, light as silk.

A change came over the man in the bed. His chest stopped moving. His mouth fell open and a stillness descended, silent as a snowflake. No longer a man, but a body, an empty shell of the person that had been.

'Gideon!'

'He's gone,' said the seated woman, her face crumpling like paper.

But he wasn't, not entirely. His spirit, his soul, was in Death's hands at the foot of the bed.

'Here,' said Death. 'Hold this.'

He placed the spirit in Valentine's arms as gently as if it were a newborn baby. It curled up like a cat against his chest, purring contentedly, not solid, yet reassuringly heavy.

'Is this that man?'

'It's the part of him that matters,' said Death. 'So be careful. Treat it with respect.'

Valentine stroked the soul, and he was sure it pushed back against his hand. 'It's warm.'

'Yes. Most of them are warm.' Death turned and began to walk down the stairs. With a long backward glance at the grieving family, Valentine followed.

At the bottom of the stairs, Death walked through the wall and out on to the street. Valentine fumbled to unlatch the door with one hand, careful not to jostle or bump the soul he was carrying. It felt strangely pleasant in his arms, comforting, and he was overwhelmed with the need to protect it. The wind whipped up Valentine's hair as he stepped out into the street, and he tucked the soul under his coat to shelter it.

Death was already on horseback and back to his full size. He held out a hand to Valentine.

'What if I drop it?'

'You won't,' said Death. He reached down with his impossibly long arms and scooped Valentine up by the armpits, sitting the boy in front of him. 'You keep that safe. I'll keep you safe.'

Valentine wrapped his arms round the bundle as Death grabbed two handfuls of Gytrash's mane.

'To the mausoleum!'

There are **many questions** about sou

which I am unable to answer, such as

'**Why?**' and '**How?**' and also '**Huh?**'

But after many years of observing souls entering and leaving the mortal world, I have learned the following:

1. Every person has a soul, even the ones who don't act like it.

2. Souls vary in size. Some are as small as a smallish house-rat. Others are as big as a biggish house-rat.

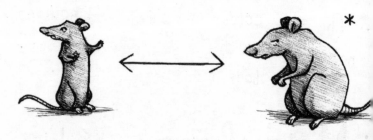

* not actual size

3. Newer souls are usually compact, dense and a little crispy around the edges. Older souls are softer and more fluid. The oldest, wateriest souls need to be collected in jars.

Greenish glow
Hefty weight
Holds together well

AVA BUTCHER

newest soul

Oozy texture
Smells like soap & strawberries

N. E. BAKER

Looks and tastes exactly like chicken soup*

C. ANDLE STICKMAKER

oldest soul

*do not taste

. The size, colour and smell of a soul have nothing to do with the size, colour and smell of the body it inhabits.

· Most of them are warm.

Six Feet Under

The ride was even more terrifying from up front, where Valentine could see the world rushing towards them at a sickening pace. The wind blew through his hair and soon the grubby buildings and carts dissolved from view, leaving only darkness up ahead. It was almost a relief.

The soul shivered and shook as though it too was fearful of this ghastly ride. Valentine held it close and whispered to it.

'Gideon Pike. Don't be frightened, Gideon Pike.'

It seemed to shift and settle in his lap, comforted, and Valentine felt better too.

Gytrash halted abruptly once again, and only Death's arm round his waist stopped Valentine from flying forward. Death lifted the boy down and dismounted behind him.

They were in a graveyard. Of course. Where else would

Death take him? Headstones and crosses were jumbled together, choked by nettles and ivy. A great weeping yew spread thick, snaking roots across the footpath, pulling up the paving slabs in chunks.

'Good lad.' Death patted the horse affectionately. 'Off you go.'

The beast ran forward, leaping and melting mid-air into a cloud of grey smoke, which was immediately swept away by the wind.

'Whoa,' said Valentine. A million and one questions bubbled under the surface, but he couldn't put them into words that made any sort of sense. His mind swirled and spun, and he wondered if he ought to sit down and put his head between his knees.

'Valentine!' Death clicked his fingers, bone on bone. 'Aren't you coming?'

'Coming where?'

'Home, of course. Home sweet home.' Death placed both hands heavily on Valentine's shoulders and turned him round.

They were standing in front of a small stone building. Two angels, carved from white stone but stained by water and moss, knelt at either side of an arched wooden door. It was secured with a huge, rusty iron padlock.

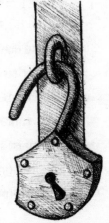

'What do you think?'

'Is it a grave?' said Valentine.

'Better. It's a mausoleum.'

'But it's a . . . it's a place for dead bodies, right?'

'Don't worry,' said Death. 'It's hardly used. And the neighbours are very quiet.' He strode forward and directly through the solid door. 'Well?' his muffled voice came from within. 'What are you waiting for?'

'Um . . . Mister Death?' Valentine really didn't want to go inside, but he wasn't all that keen on being alone outside, either. 'I can't get in.'

Death's head popped back through the door. 'Oh. Right. Silly me.' He stepped out. From his pocket he produced a large black key on a long loop of string, which he used to open the padlock. He hung it round Valentine's neck. 'Don't lose that.'

Valentine followed Death through the tomb door. A gust of wind blew a handful of early autumn leaves in behind them, and the door swung closed.

Inside the mausoleum it was very, very dark. Valentine shuffled forward until he bumped into a stone table standing waist-high in the middle of the room. Cold air seemed to radiate from the thick stone walls.

Death blew on his hand and a small flame appeared at the tip of his bony finger. He produced and lit a votive candle, shaking out his burning hand to extinguish it.

'There we go. Cosy.'

Death was stood on the opposite side of the table, which Valentine guessed was actually a plinth designed to hold a coffin. To his right and left were rectangular niches in the walls for more coffins, and smaller alcoves meant for candles. In one there was a bunch of roses, so long dead that only the cobwebs were holding it together. In another was a toothless skull, minus the bottom jaw.

The far end of the room was hidden by Death's vast shape. He was much too big, his head touching the apex of the ceiling and his wings brushing the walls on either side. The candlelight illuminated Death's skull, making strange shadows in the empty eye sockets and below the cheekbones. It seemed to have no effect on his cloak, which remained a stubborn pool of darkness.

'Make yourself at home,' said Death.

How was he supposed to do that? He was beginning to shiver from the cold of the mausoleum, or perhaps it was from the shock of the afternoon's events.

'There's a couple of crates behind you,' said Death. 'Thought you could use them as seats. Humans love sitting down, right?'

'Right,' said Valentine. With his one free hand, he placed a rough wooden box on its end and perched on the least splintery edge.

Death folded in his wings, collapsing them down like a paper lantern until they weren't there at all. 'Give me Gideon Pike.'

Reluctantly, Valentine handed over the soul. He had grown to like the weight of it and felt oddly hollow once he let it go.

'Back soon,' said Death. 'Stay here.'

'On my own?' A great shiver ran down Valentine's back, as though someone had walked over his grave. Thus far, he'd coped pretty well with all the strangeness, but sitting alone in a cold, dark tomb sounded grim. 'Can't I come with you?'

'I'll leave Atropos for company.'

'Who?'

'Come down, old girl.'

Wings fluttered behind him, and a large black crow swooped close over Valentine's head before landing on the table. She had a sharp beak, bright, questioning eyes and a single white feather in her tail.

'You'll keep an eye on him for me, won't you, Atropos?'

The bird bowed in Death's direction.

'Explore the graveyard, Valentine. Have fun. Just don't go opening any tombs.'

'Why would I—'

Death lifted the hood of his cloak up over his skull and let it fall over his face. It kept falling, and within half a second it, and he, was gone entirely.

'—open a tomb?' Valentine finished.

The candle spluttered, making their shadows dance on the walls.

'Now what?' said Valentine to the bird.

It tilted its head to the side. No help at all.

Valentine shivered. His newly issued outfit was made from thick, smart, hard-wearing wool, designed to be neat and practical for all sorts of work. But inside the stone box, away from the sunlight, it hardly seemed enough to keep the chill from his skin. He wondered where he would sleep. There was no room for a bed, no sign of any blanket. Perhaps Death never slept, but Valentine would have to.

'On second thoughts,' Valentine declared to the darkness. 'I will go outside. It might be warmer.'

He was right. It was one of those beautiful afternoons that hadn't realized it was halfway through September, and summer was already over. The sun on his neck cheered him immediately. Atropos fluttered through the doorway behind him and settled on a low branch of a nearby yew tree.

The graveyard was far bigger than the churchyard at St Pancras, the only one he had ever walked through. The mausoleum seemed to be more or less at its centre, and it spread in all directions, divided here and there by dry stone walls and iron railings, cut through with paths and hedges, punctuated with large, gloomy trees.

'I'm thirsty,' Valentine thought out loud. 'I wonder if there's a water pump somewhere.'

Atropos cawed and made a clicking noise.

'Or a well. Do they have wells in graveyards? Probably not.'

Atropos clicked again, and flew round, landing directly in front of him.

'It's as if you understand me. Surely not?' said Valentine.

The bird jerked her head in an irritated way, as if she couldn't believe he was so stupid. She took off again, flying for three or four seconds before resting on a headstone and cawing to him again.

Valentine started to walk towards her, and she moved on again, pausing only to let him catch up, and before long they had covered a considerable distance.

Every grave was different. Here a huge stone slab lay flat on the ground, every inch carved with Bible verses in neat, upright print. Beside it a large plinth stretched upwards with an angel perched on top, hands folded in prayer, the name of the occupants on the base in looping, decorative script. The next bore only a small, rough

HERE REST THE
BONES
of Jimmy
Cotton
Lying low &
feeling rotten

rock, the size of a loaf of bread, carved only with initials.

Some graves were new, with fresh earth heaped on top and covered with flowers. Others were overgrown with brambles, headstones tilted to the side like broken teeth. The oldest stones were rough from years of wind and rain. One in particular caught Valentine's eye – the

I'M
WITH
STUPID

letters were untidily jumbled together, as though the engraver had run out of time, or space, or both. Perhaps it was carved by a new apprentice, like Valentine. He wondered what his own headstone would say, then quickly buried the thought.

It wasn't the cough
That carried me off
It was the coffin
They carried me off in

Atropos came to a stop on a small arched roof sticking out from an ancient stone wall. This time she waited for Valentine to pick his way across the uneven ground.

'Water!' She'd brought him to a tiny fountain, set inside a small, temple-shaped structure that came up to shoulder-height on Valentine. Clear, cold water trickled out of a hole in the

DEAD END

33

rock, ran down well-worn channels and collected in a stone basin on the floor. 'Clever bird. You *do* understand me.'

She puffed up her chest and took a bow.

Dipping his cupped hands into the water, Valentine took a long drink and tried to take stock of his situation. 'How on earth did you end up here, Valentine?'

The crow watched him suspiciously.

'Don't look at me like that,' said Valentine. 'I'm only talking to myself because there's nobody else to talk to. I'm not used to being on my own.'

And he really needed to talk to somebody. It was too difficult to make sense of his new circumstances. Too many big questions.

'One thing at a time, Valentine. Let's see. I've left the hospital. I'm an apprentice now. I've got a master, and he seems quite friendly. I've got water, my own clothes and a couple of crates to sit on. That's more than I had this morning.'

But no bed. No human companions. No food. Then there was the small matter of all the dying. Maybe he shouldn't think too hard about that.

'I'll be fine,' he said to the bird. 'I'll do as I'm told and try not to think about the deadness of it all. Carrying souls from one place to another. Just like delivering a letter, right, girl?'

A scrabbling noise. Atropos was still on her perch, unmoving. There was no sign of anyone else in the graveyard – no one living, at least.

There it was again, the rustle of leaves, and an airy, snuffling sound like somebody breathing heavily.

'Hullo?' he called but got no reply.

There was nothing here that could harm him, he reminded himself. A graveyard was just like a garden. Except that it was full of dead people instead of flowers.

If he was to be Death's apprentice, then he couldn't afford to be fearful of wandering in a lonely graveyard. It wasn't even dark out.

'Don't worry, Atropos,' he said, summoning up some cheery courage. 'Probably a squirrel.'

Atropos shrugged her wings as if to say, *We both know it's something bigger than a squirrel.*

He took three bold steps in the direction of the noise, then paused to listen again. It was coming from behind a large raised rectangular grave.

'Who's there?' called Valentine, his words floating away on the wind. 'Show yourself.'

He crept up on the grave with small, steady steps. Valentine took a deep breath and peered round the corner.

WHUMP!

Something crashed into the back of his knees, taking his feet right out from under him.

Valentine let out a squawk as he hit the ground. The blurry shape spun and charged back towards him, and instinctively he screwed his eyes tight and covered his face.

The creature was on him in an instant. Hot, stinking breath hit Valentine's face as it panted and drooled and . . .

Licked him.

A wet tongue slathered across Valentine's hand and then his cheek. He opened one eye, cautiously.

A dog was sitting by Valentine's feet, tongue hanging out, ears cocked in a playful way.

Valentine laughed. 'Where did you come from?'

He got back to his feet, dusting off his breeches.

'There's no houses nearby,' said Valentine. 'Do you not belong to anyone?'

The dog gave a single yap.

'You can belong to me if you like.' Stooping, he scratched the top of the dog's head and it nuzzled against his hand. 'I've always wished for a pet.'

A dog could be a best friend – faithful no matter what.

Exactly what Valentine needed.

The dog noticed Atropos and bounded towards her, sniffing curiously. She took off and fluttered a few feet over to a higher perch, peering down at the mutt with disapproval. It bounded back to Valentine's side.

'What do you think, Atropos? Will Death let me keep him?'

Water, his own clothes, a couple of crates *and* a loyal furry companion. Things were getting better already.

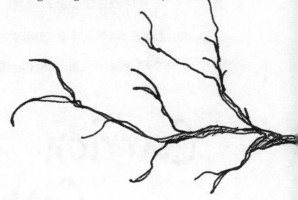

Infernal Beasts

Many strange and fearsome creatures inhabit the boundaries between life and death. Consult this useful guide before selecting a familiar, and you are sure to find your ideal otherworldly companion.

Carrion Crow

- Bird of Omen — warns mortals of their impending demise

- Traditional funereal black
- Watchful and wise
- Silent swooping flight for dramatic entrances
- Reliable as a lookout and messenger

Pale Horse

- Psychopomp – guides and transports souls on their final journey
- Noble and imposing stature

- Thunderous hoofbeats strike fear into the hearts of mortals
- Can travel through the nothingness beyond creation to avoid traffic
- Large enough to carry two human children, one old woman, a small dog and the skeletal spectre of Death, should the need arise

Graveyard Grim

- Guards the portal to the Underworld, I suppose
- Slobbery and gormless
- Annoying yappy bark
- A bit too keen on digging for a cemetery dweller
- Strong 'wet dog' smell even when dry

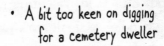

Brown Bread

eath was already in the mausoleum when Valentine went back inside.

'I brought food,' said Death, setting a cloth-wrapped bundle on the table. 'I wasn't sure what children eat.'

'Oh, the usual,' said Valentine. 'Barley gruel and a small beer. Boiled beef and vegetables. Mutton on Wednesdays; pea soup on Thursdays . . .' His stomach rumbled in response. Foundling food had been plain and repetitive, but his belly had always been full, and as the matron reminded them every morning and night, not everyone was as lucky.

'I brought you bread,' said Death.

'Bread's good, too!' said Valentine quickly. He hastily unwrapped the bundle – a small brown loaf, still warm, and in a jar – 'Real butter! Thank you!'

He dived on the food, ravenous from his day of strange adventure, but the matron's voice popped into his head: 'Manners, manners, manners!'

'Will you be having some, Mister . . . um . . . sir?'

'No, it's all for you.'

There was no knife, so Valentine tore the bread into chunks and messily pressed the butter on with his fingers, which he licked clean. He ate fast, taking big bites. Death perched on the edge of the table and looked pleased with himself.

'I've never had to look after a living human before,' he said. 'Keeping people alive, it's not really my area of knowledge. You'll have to tell me if there's anything you need. I want you to be content.'

Valentine ate most of the bread and butter, and then made himself stop even though his stomach was still rumbling. He took the crust over to the door of the mausoleum and opened it.

'Here, boy,' he called, and the little dog was there in an instant, tail wagging furiously. 'Here you go.'

He threw the bread, which the dog swallowed in a single bite.

'I found him in the graveyard,' said Valentine. 'He must be lost. Can I keep him?'

Atropos cawed in protest from her dark corner.

'Well . . .' said Death.

Valentine scooped up the dog, and the two of them looked

at Death hopefully. 'I'll take good care of him. You'll hardly know he's here.'

'I suppose it's good for you to have a familiar, in our line of work.' Death rubbed his bony brow. 'Though a crow or a rook is more traditional.'

Atropos fluttered down to the ground beneath them. She flapped her wings and hopped about angrily.

'He'll keep me company when you're gone.' The dog licked Valentine's face in agreement.

'You can keep him,' said Death. 'He'll have to stay here when you're going on collections, though. We can't have a dog getting underfoot while we work.'

'Thank you.' Valentine beamed.

The dog yapped happily and leaped out of Valentine's arms before settling down for a good scratch.

'You'll need to choose a name for him. Something with a bit of dignity and gravitas. Fenrir. Or Varkolak.'

'Or Fluffy,' said Valentine. 'Or Scraps. Ooh! What about Captain Bones?' The dog nuzzled against Valentine's legs. He reached down to stroke his fur, and then shivered. 'He'll keep me warmer at night, too.'

'Warm.' Death clicked his fingers. 'That was the other thing. Fed and warm. I never notice the cold, personally.' He looked for inspiration, but there was nothing in the mausoleum that could bring any warmth – nowhere to build a fire or boil a kettle. 'Ah.'

He grasped the edge of his cloak and began to tear it. It ripped as easily as paper, a large rectangle falling away. He held it up, measuring it against Valentine.

'That should do you.' He swooped the fabric over Valentine's head and deftly tied it round his neck in a fatherly gesture. Or at least, what Valentine imagined a fatherly gesture must be like, having never had a father himself.

Immediately he felt warmer. His nostrils were filled with the dusty odour of smoke, and a metallic smell so strong he could taste pennies.

Death straightened up and shook out his cloak, which showed no sign of any tear. 'It will help you blend in.'

'You don't think a boy in a huge black cloak will stand out even more?'

'It's not black,' said Death. 'Your human eyes can't see the true colour, so your gaze slides away from it. Very useful for wandering unnoticed. And you'll always win at hide-and-seek.'

'Thank you.' Valentine swished the cloak, enjoying the heaviness on his shoulders. It would do as both winter coat and blanket. He settled himself down into one of the lowest coffin niches. It might do as a sort of bed if he wrapped himself up tightly in his cloak. Maybe he could get some straw from somewhere to use as a mattress. Maybe, just maybe this could all become somehow bearable . . .

'What are you doing?' said Death. 'Work to be done. Come on.'

What followed was an overwhelming high-speed tour of all the best dying spots in London. Gytrash was summoned again, and Valentine was spirited from place to place as Death made his collections. First, an army captain who was determined to meet his maker standing up, his empty corpse remaining balanced upright with one arm on the mantel as they retreated from his rooms. Next, an elderly nun patiently cared for by the other sisters. A man who'd made a drunken

bet that he could swallow a billiard ball only to realize, too late, that he could not. A sailor drowned before his ship had even left the harbour. A woman carried away by a severely infected tooth, who insisted that she wouldn't go with them unless they granted her last wish.

'You don't have a choice,' said Death.

'You'll never catch me,' the woman snapped.

'I absolutely will,' said Death. 'One hundred and fourteen seconds from now, your heart stops beating.'

'I'll fight you off.'

'Not without a heart, you won't.'

The woman shook her fist at Death, but it was a feeble gesture and the effort made her groan.

'One hundred and fourteen seconds,' said Valentine. 'That's nearly two minutes.'

'One hundred and ten, now,' said Death.

'That might be long enough, mightn't it? To do her last wish.'

Death sighed. 'I don't get involved with last wishes any more. Too much trouble. And they're rarely as good as you'd expect.'

'Please?'

'As you wish.' Death sat down at the foot of the bed. 'A minute and a half, Eleanor. Long enough to make a confession, write a love letter, say a prayer . . . What will it be?'

'My wig. Pass me my wig.' She pointed weakly to a dressing table where an enormous pink-powdered wig rested on a wooden head-shaped stand.

'Your . . . wig?' Valentine couldn't help asking.

'Yes. I need to look my best when they find me.'

'See what I mean?' said Death.

Valentine picked up the wig, which was much heavier than he'd expected and smelled of sour milk and sweat.

'Hurry up, boy!' the woman hissed. 'Put it on me.'

Death shook his head and folded his arms.

Valentine scrabbled to get the awkward woolly mass on to her head. She had very little of her own hair left, and what was there was limp and brittle.

'Make sure it's the right way round!'

Close up, her skin appeared fragile too, pitted and saggy. It hadn't been obvious from the other side of the room because of the candlelight, and because she was covered in a very thick layer of chalk-white make-up.

'I suppose I'm lucky, really –' she said, as Valentine passed her a small hand-mirror – 'to go before my youthful good looks fade. Don't tell anyone . . .' She dropped her voice even lower, forcing Valentine to lean in. 'But I'm almost twenty-six.'

'Twenty-six?!' Valentine blinked. She might have been seventy-six by the state of her.

She took his surprise as a compliment. 'I know. Most people don't think me a day over twenty-one.'

'It's the make-up,' said Death in response to Valentine's baffled expression. 'Incredibly poisonous. They get sick from it, then they use more to cover it and . . . Time's up, Eleanor.'

'One last thing,' she said, as Death's fingers found the edges of her soul above her cheekbones. 'How do I look?'

'Beautiful,' said Death, and pulled the soul free. 'For a corpse. Onwards, Valentine.'

'Is it always this busy?' Valentine panted as they hurried back out to where Gytrash was waiting.

'Busy?' said Death. 'This is a quiet day.'

'It is?'

Death paused. 'You're tired. Am I right?'

Valentine didn't want his master to think he was lazy. 'A little bit.'

'Aha.' Death tucked the newly acquired soul into his cloak. 'Living humans take so much maintenance. But I'll get used to it. How often is it you need to sleep?'

'Every day.'

'*Every* day? How terribly boring for you.'

'Not really,' said Valentine, 'because we're asleep, so we don't notice. Once you fall asleep, it's like you open your eyes and eight hours have passed.'

'Eight HOURS?'

'Thereabouts.'

'Eight hours *every day?!*' He climbed up on to the horse. 'That means you've spent about four years of your life asleep, already.'

'Or more,' said Valentine. 'Babies sleep longer.'

Death offered his arm to Valentine, who was already

47

getting used to being hauled off his feet and on to Gytrash's back. 'No wonder you lot keep coming back for more lifetimes. You barely have time to get anything done. We'll have to make some adjustments to your workload.'

'We what?'

'We'll make some adjustments, on account of your pathetic mortal body. I mustn't work you to death. Work you to death . . . Ha! Get it?'

'No, the bit about coming back for more lifetimes? What do you mean?'

Death twisted in the saddle and pulled his hood back to face Valentine. 'Oh. Goodness. I forgot. You don't know anything at all yet, do you?'

Care and Fee

If you have spent a few thousand years amongst the **dead**, you may not be aware of the tremendous effort involved in **living**. Should you find yourself responsible for keeping a mortal alive, here are the basic facts.

Oxygen – humans require a constant supply of oxygen. Never store your mortal in an airtight vault and ensure your catacombs are well ventilated.

air holes

for cadavers only

blood in here = good

blood out here = bad

Blood – your mortal contains a large amount of blood, which must remain on *the inside* of their bod. If red liquid begins leaking from your human, they require urgent repair.

Squishy bits –

inside all mortal bodies lies a complicated jumble of soft, gooey pieces called 'organs'.

ing (of Mortals)

Organs are extremely fragile, so try not to drop or compress your human.

N.B. Although revolting, these squishy bits are necessary and should NOT be removed.

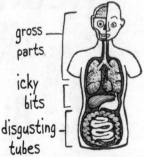

gross parts

icky bits

disgusting tubes

Food and water - humans need feeding and watering several times a day, and they think of little else. Encourage your mortal to eat green things - they are likely to resist. Warning: not all green things are food.

FOOD

cabbage

pea soup

pears

NOT FOOD

toad

holly

glass

Warmth - mortals are fussy about temperature. If they are too hot, or too cold, they will show their displeasure by dying. Provide clothing and blankets, and avoid contact with naked flames.

No

Also no

Reunited with the Ancestors

The next three weeks blurred together. Death swept Valentine Crow from place to place, gathering souls at every stop, each one a little different, each ending unique. When they weren't at somebody's bedside, they were galloping along on Gytrash's back, or trailing through ink-black tunnels beneath the London streets.

He did his best to keep up, but eventually Death would notice Valentine's stifled yawns and drop him off at the mausoleum to sleep.

Huddled into a coffin niche, wrapped in a cloak belonging to the Grim Reaper and snuggled by a dog long overdue for a bath: it wasn't the most comfortable of lodgings, but by the time Valentine lay down he was too exhausted to care.

For a boy who had lived most of his life in the same place,

doing the same things, it was a dizzying whirl. So many faces, places, stories. So many questions that he never found time to ask.

Each day he opened his eyes into a waking world far stranger than his dreams. It took a moment to become aware of the cold stone at his back and the snoring dog curled up against his belly and gradually remember where he was. It took a few more moments to believe it.

But one morning, exactly one month into his apprenticeship, he woke without the usual confusion. Things were starting to feel normal.

Lying in the darkness, he counted on his fingers, trying to work out what date it was, then sat up sharply. Captain Bones slumped gracelessly on to the floor and startled himself awake.

'Sorry, Bones.'

The dog huffed grumpily.

'It's my birthday today,' said Valentine.

In fact, the Foundling Hospital hadn't marked birthdays – there were far too many children, and they were much too busy with the business of keeping them all fed and well behaved. But there was something magical about the idea of a birthday. It was an achievement, to survive another whole year in this world. So, when Philomena told him that they had arrived at the hospital on the same day, they decided they would count that as their birthday. And they would always find a way to slip each other a little note or gift on the day.

Last year he'd given her a silver button he'd found in the courtyard – probably dropped by a visitor come to marvel at the unfortunate orphans – and she'd brought him half a scone, smuggled from the kitchen when she was washing up from the governors' tea.

Valentine wondered where she was. He wondered if Philomena thought of him this morning, too.

Stiff from sleeping on cold stone, he was glad to get to his feet, careful not to step on Captain Bones's tail in the gloom. 'Time to face the day, then.'

Captain Bones got up to stretch, nails clicking on the slabs, already panting as though he had run a mile.

'Hush. Listen.'

Outside there were voices. The words weren't clear enough to make out, but he instantly recognized the low, gravelly tone of Death. The other was a woman; he had never heard her before. In this whole month, Valentine had never seen another person in the graveyard. He stood up and listened at the door. Captain Bones put his nose to the doorframe and had a good sniff, his tail wagging all the while.

A peal of raucous laughter fed Valentine's curiosity, and he summoned his courage and stepped outside.

Death and his visitor were deep in conversation on the other side of the footpath. Death was perched on top of a

54

narrow headstone, the woman on a tree stump with her short legs dangling. Atropos sat contentedly on the woman's shoulder, tugging playfully at the string on her cap. All three looked up when Valentine emerged.

'There you are!' said Death with what sounded like relief. 'I came to check on you an hour ago and it was like trying to wake the dead, so I thought I'd let you rest.'

'This be him, then, eh?' said the woman. She was old-ish, white-haired with grizzled features, short and solidly built. 'Small for such a big job.'

'More than a match for it,' said Death. 'Taking it all in his stride. Big plans for today.'

"S'av a proper look-see then.' She beckoned Valentine over and he stood politely in front of her.

Valentine knew how to behave for this sort of inspection. Stand straight, speak softly, remember your manners.

He made a neat little bow. 'Pleased to meet you.'

The woman's hand shot out, quicker than a frog's tongue, and grabbed his arm. She looped her hand round his wrist so her thumb and middle finger touched and held it aloft.

She tutted. 'He's thinner than you are. What are you feeding him?'

'Bread, mostly.' Death rubbed the back of his head defensively. 'And butter.'

'Is that all?'

'I'm new to this!'

Atropos clucked.

'You always take her side,' said Death.

'Got all your teeth, lad?'

Valentine nodded and bared his teeth in a grimace. She hooked one finger right into his mouth to get a better view. He let out an involuntary squeak of alarm. She tugged each of his ears, turning his head from side to side, then took hold of his chin and stared intently into his eyes from an uncomfortably close position.

'Good enough condition,' she said, finally releasing him. 'You could have picked a worse one.'

'I didn't pick him,' said Death. 'I just got the one I was given. No offence, Valentine.'

'None taken,' said Valentine. 'I didn't pick you either.'

The woman gave a gleeful chuckle. 'With this one I give you . . . fifty-fifty odds of succeeding.'

'Succeeding at what?' said Valentine.

'*If* you feed him properly.'

'Yes, yes, all right, you miserable old hag – you've made your point.'

Valentine expected the woman to be upset by this, but she cackled with ominous laughter. Death began searching through the pockets of his cloak and the lady gave Valentine a sly wink.

'Here. Hands out,' said Death. Valentine did as he was told, and Death dropped a few coins into them. 'Go and buy yourself some food. You can show him to the market,' he added to the woman. 'Since you're leaving anyway.'

'Aye.' She heaved herself on to her feet with a groan. 'There's only so much of you I can face in one lifetime. Ha ha!'

'Got your key, Valentine?'

Valentine patted his chest where the reassuringly heavy key was tucked safely into his shirt.

'She'll show you a quick route to town. Be sure to lock the gate behind you. I can't have humans in the graveyard.'

'Too late for that,' said the woman.

'You hardly count as human,' said Death as the woman turned her back on them and began walking through the rows of graves with a stiff but determined limp. She reminded Valentine of those stories about battle-hardened pirate captains, weathered by storms and missing a few body parts from swordfights, but fierce and powerful, nonetheless.

'Get after her, then, Val. Buy whatever you want – money's no use to me. And then hurry back. I've got a present for you.'

Valentine's heart jumped. 'A birthday present?'

'Is it your birthday?'

'I think so . . .'

'Oh,' said Death. 'Then I suppose it is a birthday present.'

'I'm leaving!' shouted the woman, already surprisingly far away.

Valentine ran after her, then slowed to match her pace once he caught up. They walked in silence for a few moments, then took a sharp right turn.

'It's big, isn't it?' said Valentine. 'Where are we? I can't even see a church.'

'See that grave with the anchor?' She pointed. 'That's where you turn left to get to my exit. Remember that. I'm sure you'll be plaguing my corner of town, like your master.'

'Excuse me for asking,' said Valentine. 'But, when he said you're not human . . . that was a joke, right? You're a person? And not one of . . . whatever he is?'

'A person, yes. A human, probably. One of his sort, definitely not.'

'How do you know him?'

'We go back a long way. A long, long way.'

'It's strange for a person to be friends with Death.'

'I wouldn't exactly call us friends.'

They reached an iron railing, ten feet tall, topped with spikes. Beyond the gates were only open meadows and hillsides retreating into the distance.

'This can't be London,' Valentine muttered. He took out his key and unlocked the gate, pulling it back.

'It isn't,' said the woman, stepping through. 'But this is.'

Valentine stepped through behind her, on to a cobbled street.

He looked back at the gate he'd just come through. It was overgrown with brambles and ivy as though nobody had opened it for a very long time. Beyond lay a graveyard, but not *his* graveyard. It was one of those tiny city churchyards where soil had been piled up over the years to make space for more burials, until the whole thing was much higher than the street below. The gate was set within precariously leaning stone walls, with weed-tangled steps leading upwards.

Valentine had not walked down any steps. He turned and stepped back through the gate. Back in his own graveyard, the chain-and-anchor statue visible in the distance. The sky beyond the railings wide and empty.

He stepped through again. Back to the cobbled street.

He understood now why Death had told him to lock the gate behind him. Whatever their graveyard was, *wherever* it was, it was anything but ordinary.

'What . . . ? How . . . ?'

'Forgive me for not getting overly excited. I have business to attend to, so listen carefully. Follow this street. Take the second left. First right. Through the arched alleyway, left and right again, and you're at the market. Got it?'

Valentine nodded. 'Maybe?'

'Get some cheese – you need some fat on those bones. But

59

not from the man with the blue cart; he'll charge you double what it's worth.'

'Thank you,' said Valentine.

'And eat something green!'

He could smell the market before he could see it. The usual London stench of horses and smoke and the filth of thousands of humans packed into too-small streets – but now other smells too, more tempting and unusual. Something salty, meaty, fishy. Something earthy and hot and pleasantly bitter. Something sweet and spicy and deliciously familiar – what was it? He tried to focus on that one smell amongst all the

others, to find the memory it was pointing to.

He'd always had enough to eat at the hospital, but day after day it would be the same thing. And Death, though he meant well, had no idea about food and flavours, so meals had been mostly bread and butter for the last month. Now Valentine had money in his pocket, and he could choose whatever he wanted.

A man sold whole pigs' trotters, which smelled like Easter dinner but looked like, well, trotters. Glistening oysters sat in their shimmering shells, like fairy dinner plates, and Valentine plucked up the courage to try them, only to recoil from the smell once he got close. Eels in jelly neither looked nor smelled appealing, though the men at the stall evidently thought they were fit for the king's table. Potatoes, sold by the pound or by the sack, seemed a safer choice, but he had no idea what to do with them. The graveyard didn't have a kitchen and he wasn't sure how to build a fire, or what to do with it once he had one.

He stared blankly as the people bustled past him, talking, joking, arguing, rushing, and thought how effortlessly they all belonged to this world. They understood how it worked. They knew what to do.

That smell again – *gingerbread*. That's what it was! He'd get some gingerbread. Once he bought *something*, he was sure it would get easier. His very first time buying something just for him, that he wouldn't have to share. He pushed back his cloak in order to be seen better and cleared his throat.

'I'd like some gingerbread, please?'

"Course, darlin. How much?'

'Ummm . . .' He held his fingers a few inches apart. 'This much?'

'Are you a simpleton? Penny's worth? Halfpenny?'

'Oh. A penny's worth, please.' He shuffled his feet awkwardly as the woman cut him a slab and handed it over, wrapped in butcher's paper.

'Valentine?' A voice from behind him.

He shoved the gingerbread into the pocket of his cloak, afraid for half a moment that someone would take it away from him.

'I knew it was you!' A girl with a huge basket in her arms and an equally huge grin on her face stood facing him.

'Philomena – I can't believe it!' He blinked in surprise. And on their birthday too.

'Quite a style you've got there,' she said, nodding towards his cloak.

He tugged at his cuffs and smoothed his hand over his collar, embarrassed that he was walking the streets in Death's odd, blacker-than-black attire.

She shifted her basket to the other hip. 'Didn't know you were off to become a dandy. Makes my laundry basket look all the more shabby.'

Valentine swished the cloak dramatically over his shoulders and bowed low to cover his awkwardness.

Philomena laughed and blew a stray lock of hair out of her eyes. 'Are you living near here, then?'

'. . . Sort of.' He wasn't sure how he could explain exactly where, and he hoped she wouldn't ask.

'I'm round the corner at Mercy Dyer's.' She jerked her head to indicate the direction. 'Midwife – so they say – does a bit of everything as far as I can tell. Beer brewing. Mending. Laundry.' She lifted the basket up to illustrate her point. 'She's all right and the food isn't bad. Mad as a box of frogs, though. Likes folks to call her "Mother Mercy"!'

'Least you're not emptying the rich people's chamber pots.'

'That's the truth! Imagine what it'll be like, seeing a baby come into the world! I don't know whether I'm looking forward to it or not. She's kept me plenty busy, though, I can tell you. I'll sleep like the dead tonight!'

Valentine felt a rush of delight to have found Philomena. Somebody who understood what it was like to go from Foundling to apprentice. Somebody from the normal world of the living, who wasn't entrusting him with magic keys and the souls of the dead. Someone with a big, warm smile and plenty to say for herself.

'What are you, then?' she said. 'A funeral mute?'

'I . . . er . . .'

'It was a joke,' said Philomena. 'Because you're not talking, and the black cloak and whatnot.'

What should he tell her? He didn't want to scare her away

by telling the truth. If she'd even believe the truth, anyway.

She gasped. 'Go on, don't tell me you're working for an undertaker?'

Valentine nodded. 'It's a bit like that, yeah . . .'

'What are the chances?' She laughed. 'Me bringing people into the world and you seeing them out again! That's a good jest, isn't it?'

Maybe she wouldn't be scared away. Suddenly he needed to tell someone about all the incredible things he had witnessed in the last few weeks.

'It's Death,' he blurted out.

'What is?'

'It—he is. My master. He's Death. I'm apprentice to Death.'

Philomena's eyes widened. She leaned in and whispered, 'What, the hangman? Are you an executioner's apprentice? That's an awful thing to make you do. That shouldn't be allowed!'

'No, no!' Valentine shouldn't have said anything, but he couldn't stop now. 'Not the hangman. Actual Death. The Grim Reaper. The skeleton with the cloak and the big . . . you know, the big cutty thing!' To demonstrate his point, he pulled the back of his cloak up over his head, the way Death always looked in old paintings.

Philomena laughed and playfully nudged his shoulder with her basket. 'What is it really?'

'That's it. Really. We've been going through London,

64

taking people's souls out of their bodies right when they die.'

'Oh yeah?' She shifted her grip on the basket and put her free hand on her hip. 'And I suppose you've been flying them up to the pearly gates, too?'

'No, there's no . . .' He frowned. 'I'm not actually sure yet, where they go.'

'All right, Valentine. You need to work your story out better next time, if you want to make me your fool.'

'I'm telling the truth; I'll prove it.'

'Go on, then.'

He blinked. 'I'm not really sure how to prove it right now . . .'

'I'd better run,' said Philomena. 'There's a list a mile long I need to finish today. Can't go making a poor impression so soon in our apprenticeships, can we?'

'Right,' said Valentine, disappointed. 'Of course.'

'See you around.' She gave a little wave, adjusted her burden once more and headed off.

He had even forgotten to mention their birthday . . .

'Philomena!' he shouted after her.

She stopped and turned, expectantly.

'Happy birthday.' He unwrapped the gingerbread, broke it in half and gave her some.

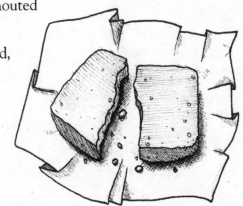

She smiled. 'Thanks – happy birthday to you too. I don't have anything to give you. We've got lovely pears at home, though. Come and find me if your master lets you out again.' She started walking again. 'Partridge Street. Mercy Dyer,' she called back. 'There's a huge tree in the yard. You can't miss it.'

Ran out of Time

After somehow purchasing himself two days' worth of food, plus a mutton bone for his dog, Valentine headed back through the cemetery gate. He was struck by a mixture of elation and loneliness. It was going to be hard to make new friends, living in a deserted cemetery.

'Hurry up!' From way across the graveyard, Death was waving both hands over his head and calling to him. 'You've been ages!'

Valentine shook himself from his thoughts and hurried back towards the mausoleum. Halfway there, Captain Bones joined him and jogged along beside him with happy yips. Bones had proved to be an excellent companion. He didn't care that he lived in a graveyard.

'Finally!' said Death, standing outside the mausoleum entrance.

'Sorry,' said Valentine. 'I didn't know how to . . . everything.'

'Never mind, you're here now. Close your eyes and hold your hands out.' Death rocked back on his bony heels, gleefully.

Valentine did as he was told. Death placed something small and heavy and crinkly in his hands.

'Open them!'

'Oh . . . Thank you?' said Valentine. He was holding a small bundle of leaves tied with twine.

'Birthday present! I've never got involved with birthdays before. It's quite fun, this whole *living* business.' Death was clearly pleased with himself, so Valentine tried to act excited about a gift of dead leaves.

'Wow,' he said. 'I love all the different . . . colours.' The leaves were all varying degrees of dead, some dry and crispy and others damp and mulchy. He turned the gift over in his hands. 'I'll have to find somewhere safe to keep them.'

'The leaves aren't the gift, silly!' said Death. 'That's the wrapping. That's what you do with birthday presents. You wrap them up. I didn't have any paper, so, I made do.'

'Ohhhhh,' said Valentine. He tugged one end of the twine and the bow unfurled. Layers of leaves fell away as he unwrapped the string.

It was a pocket watch, similar to Death's, but a little smaller, and this one was silver instead of gold. The surface was etched

with the words MEMENTO MORI. Valentine pressed the circular button that stuck out from the top, and with a pleasing clunk, it sprung open like a clamshell into two equal halves.

'Wow!' he said, and this time he meant it. 'For me? Really? Thank you.' Watches were expensive – Valentine never expected to own one.

'Every good apprentice needs his own set of tools, eventually, and I think you're ready,' said Death. 'This will help you find the souls you need to take.'

The souls you need to take. Cold panic sank down from his scalp at the reminder that he would be taking souls, and warm satisfaction surged up from his feet from knowing that Death was pleased with him. The two emotions met behind his belly button and bubbled together, excitedly. There could only be one question. 'How?'

Pay Close Attention

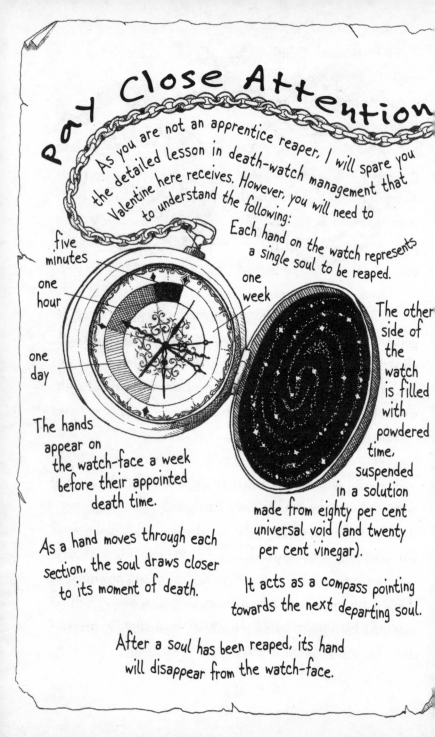

As you are not an apprentice reaper, I will spare you the detailed lesson in death-watch management that Valentine here receives. However, you will need to understand the following:

Each hand on the watch represents a single soul to be reaped.

five minutes

one hour

one week

one day

The other side of the watch is filled with powdered time, suspended in a solution made from eighty per cent universal void (and twenty per cent vinegar).

The hands appear on the watch-face a week before their appointed death time.

As a hand moves through each section, the soul draws closer to its moment of death.

It acts as a compass pointing towards the next departing soul.

After a soul has been reaped, its hand will disappear from the watch-face.

'Got it?' said Death, after a long and complicated explanation of how to read the pocket watch.

Valentine stared intently at the watch-face, counting out the sections. A hand, black with an arrowhead point and a small, decorative circle halfway down, was in the dark grey section. *The hour-of-death section.* A quaking began in Valentine's ribcage. Not fear, exactly, but . . . 'That one's going to be soon, right?' Very soon, in fact. The black hand had already travelled through three-quarters of the hour section. He jumped to his feet. 'What do I do?'

'Tap on the compass side,' said Death. 'Hold it flat.'

The compass side was filled with a deep purple-blue liquid, gently swirling beneath the glass. Tilting it disturbed fine particles that had settled on the bottom. Tiny, luminescent gold flecks billowed up and mixed with the liquid in shimmering eddies and spirals.

Valentine tapped gently on the glass. 'Nothing's happen . . . Oh!'

The gold dust within gathered together until it formed a ball, like a miniature star suspended in its own tiny night sky. After a few seconds, the star drifted forward and to the left, settling at the very edge of its enclosure.

'Due west for now,' said Death. 'Come on, then.'

Valentine hesitated, hoping for more instructions, but his mentor folded his arms, so Valentine began walking in the direction the compass was pointing. He watched the liquid carefully, wondering if there was any way to get something more helpful, like an address or a map. The star shifted and adjusted its position at the edge of the circular glass as Valentine weaved between gravestones and trees.

'How do I know how far away it is?'

'You'll get used to it,' said Death. 'Every watch has its own little quirks. We'll have to find out as we go along. An apprentice watch will only send you to deaths that are reasonably nearby anyway. Let me see.'

Valentine paused while Death took out his own watch and held it next to Valentine's. In response, Death's watch began to swirl and shimmer, too. Instead of forming into a ball, the substance within arranged itself into rows of dots and circles.

'I see,' he said. 'There's a short cut.'

'Wait,' said Valentine. Death was already striding away through the cemetery, and he hurried to keep up, hopping over cracked stones and fallen branches. 'What were all those symbols? How did you know where we're going?'

'Patience, Valentine! I'm glad that you're eager, but there's a reason that an apprenticeship takes seven years. You can't expect to understand everything right away.'

The heel of Valentine's boot slipped into a rabbit hole and he almost lost his balance. He closed the watch for safety and tucked it into the pocket of his coat, clipping the end of the chain to a buttonhole. How extremely grown-up and sophisticated.

'Come on!' Death shouted, and Valentine ran to catch up.

They came to a stop before a raised stone crypt. It had probably been very grand and expensive when it was first erected, but now the carvings had worn smooth and the ground it stood on had shifted and moved. As a result, the slab on one end had fallen and cracked, leaving a square opening.

'After you,' said Death. 'Don't worry. The coffins are underground. The stone part is just an empty box, for decoration. In we go.'

Valentine crouched down and peered into the gloom. 'You've got to be kidding.'

'Nope,' said Death, and he gave Valentine a little nudge with his foot, knocking him off balance and tipping him in through the gap.

Valentine screwed up his eyes and brought his hands across his face, anticipating a mouth full of dead leaves and dirt or even worse. Instead, he slithered down a steep slope on his belly, head first.

'Hey!' he shouted up from the bottom, scrambling to his feet and dusting himself off. 'That wasn't very nice.'

'Sorry,' said Death, clambering down to meet him. 'Mustn't be late to your first appointment.' He swept right past Valentine, blending perfectly into the darkness as he got further from the entrance.

Once again Valentine found himself struggling to keep up,

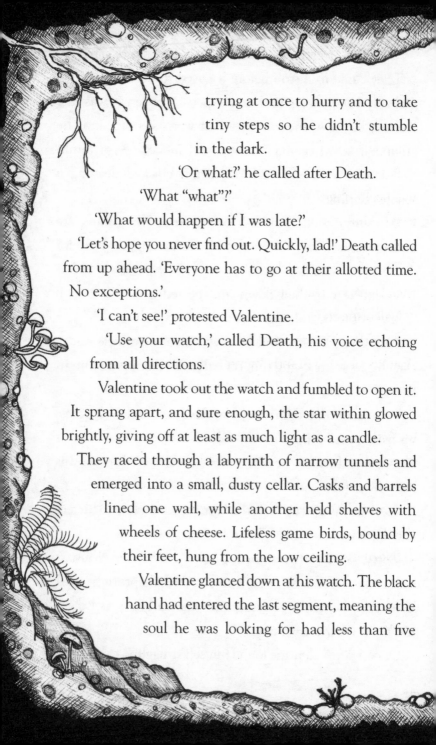

trying at once to hurry and to take
tiny steps so he didn't stumble
in the dark.

'Or what?' he called after Death.

'What "what"?'

'What would happen if I was late?'

'Let's hope you never find out. Quickly, lad!' Death called
from up ahead. 'Everyone has to go at their allotted time.
No exceptions.'

'I can't see!' protested Valentine.

'Use your watch,' called Death, his voice echoing
from all directions.

Valentine took out the watch and fumbled to open it.
It sprang apart, and sure enough, the star within glowed
brightly, giving off at least as much light as a candle.

They raced through a labyrinth of narrow tunnels and
emerged into a small, dusty cellar. Casks and barrels
lined one wall, while another held shelves with
wheels of cheese. Lifeless game birds, bound by
their feet, hung from the low ceiling.

Valentine glanced down at his watch. The black
hand had entered the last segment, meaning the
soul he was looking for had less than five

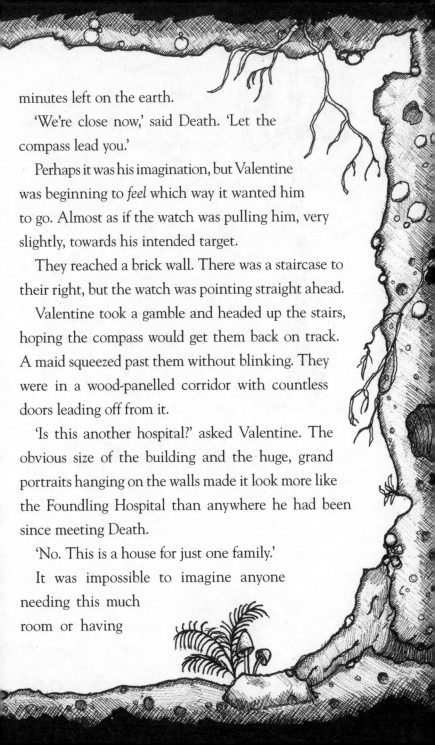

minutes left on the earth.

'We're close now,' said Death. 'Let the compass lead you.'

Perhaps it was his imagination, but Valentine was beginning to *feel* which way it wanted him to go. Almost as if the watch was pulling him, very slightly, towards his intended target.

They reached a brick wall. There was a staircase to their right, but the watch was pointing straight ahead.

Valentine took a gamble and headed up the stairs, hoping the compass would get them back on track. A maid squeezed past them without blinking. They were in a wood-panelled corridor with countless doors leading off from it.

'Is this another hospital?' asked Valentine. The obvious size of the building and the huge, grand portraits hanging on the walls made it look more like the Foundling Hospital than anywhere he had been since meeting Death.

'No. This is a house for just one family.'

It was impossible to imagine anyone needing this much room or having

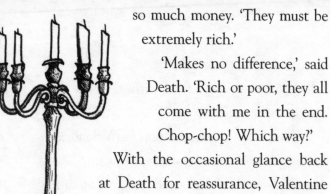

so much money. 'They must be extremely rich.'

'Makes no difference,' said Death. 'Rich or poor, they all come with me in the end. Chop-chop! Which way?'

With the occasional glance back at Death for reassurance, Valentine followed the compass down the corridor and up two more sweeping flights of stairs.

'Where is everyone?' said Valentine. He was getting nervous as the watch ticked closer. 'It's so quiet.'

'I think they're all out to watch the duel.'

Valentine stopped. 'A duel? Like, pistols at ten paces?'

'Don't get too excited. It won't be as pretty as you're imagining.'

Mortally Wounded

A final, smaller staircase took them to a flat roof bordered with a low decorative wall like the top of a castle. Twenty or so people formed a circle and at their centre, two women stared each other down.

'Ladies fighting?' said Valentine. 'I thought only men had duels.'

'Women can do anything men can do, given the opportunity,' said Death.

A woman in a pink dress pointed a finger across the circle, the large ripples of lace on her sleeve catching the breeze. 'Lucretia King is a scoundrel and a shame on her family.'

The woman opposite her stepped forward. Her white hair was piled so high on her head that she appeared much taller than her accuser, though in fact she was both younger

77

and smaller. 'And my darling cousin, Constantia, is a liar and a thief.'

'Isn't anyone going to stop them?' said Valentine.

'Oh, don't worry,' a young footman whispered without taking his eyes off the action. 'They do this all the time. It's the third duel this month. They'll be friends again by teatime.'

'I don't think so,' muttered Valentine. One of them wasn't going to have any more tea, ever.

'Miss King shall choose the weapon,' announced a man in red livery.

'I choose rapiers. You never were good at fencing, Connie!'

A wave of queasiness washed over Valentine. He clutched Death's cloak to steady himself, and Death placed a hand on his shoulder. It felt more reassuring than a skeleton hand should.

'Wait,' he whispered. 'Is one of them going to be run through with a sword?' Duels were thrilling in stories, but this real-life scene turned his stomach. He didn't want to see blood spilled.

'No,' said Death. 'The aim is to be the first to draw blood. A single scratch and the duel will be over, the winner decided.'

Valentine breathed out heavily in relief, momentarily forgetting why he was there. 'All right.'

The servant offered two swords to Lucretia, who selected one and waved it in front of her, testing the weight, staring

down the length of the blade to
check the shape of it. Constantia
snatched up the other, and the two
women took their starting positions.
The onlookers stepped back.

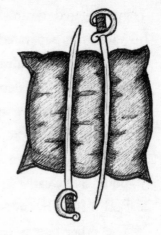

'On my word,' said the servant.
'Three, two, one . . .'

Lucretia lunged forward,
jabbing the sword at her cousin.
Her first strike was successful,
scratching across the back of Constantia's hand. A thin line
of blood bloomed up over the skin. Constantia howled.

'First blood!' shouted the servant. He stepped forward,
arms out to encourage the two women apart.

'But if it's only a scratch, why are we here?' said Valentine.

'She cheated!' shouted Constantia. 'I wasn't ready!'

'Don't you dare call me a cheat, you witch,' hissed Lucretia.
She threw down her sword and pushed the sleeves of her blue
silk dress up to her elbows.

Some of the servants had already lost interest and began
to shuffle back indoors.

'I knew you couldn't be trusted, you common rat!'

'Common?!'

Both women were shouting over each other. Constantia
grabbed Lucretia by the hair, and Lucretia swung a punch.
Constantia caught her arm and the two of them stumbled.

They staggered towards the edge of the roof and the knee-high wall that separated them from the fall.

'No!' Valentine realized what was about to happen.

Death covered Valentine's eyes. There was a strangled yell, and a collective gasp from the onlookers, and when he removed his hands, the women were gone.

'Which one of them . . . ?'

'Both,' said Death.

'Both?! But why isn't my watch showing two hands?'

'The other one is on mine.' He sighed. 'And now we have to trudge all the way back downstairs; I hate it when that happens.'

Valentine took a deep breath before following. On the paving by the grand front door, the two women lay in a tangle of dresses. Constantia's leg was obviously broken – even beneath the layers of petticoats, Valentine could see that it lay at an unnatural angle. Lucretia had landed face up, her eyes wide open as a pool of dark red blood spread across the rocks beneath her head.

'This isn't over,' said Constantia.

'It definitely is,' said Death.

'Excuse me,' said Lucretia with a note of disdain in her voice. 'We're in the middle of something here.'

'No,' said Death. 'You're very much at the end of something. Your life, to be exact.'

'Who are you?' said Constantia.

Death threw his hands up. 'I'm Death. Obviously. Who else could I be?'

'Take her, then,' said Lucretia. 'Because I won the duel.'

'You're both coming with me,' said Death.

'Then take her first. I'll have the last word.'

'Yes,' said Constantia. 'I really ought to go first because I outrank her.'

'How dare you!' said Lucretia. 'I've changed my mind. Take me first.'

'I'm not going to wherever she's going,' said Constantia.

'Enough!' said Death. 'Shut up, both of you!'

The worried face of a servant peered out from the window

above. 'Oh, my lord,' he said, and disappeared from view.

'This is your moment, Valentine. Which one is yours?'

'How do I know?'

'The watch, of course.' Death reached a skeletal arm over Valentine's shoulder and tapped sharply on the glass of his watch. The golden dust separated from the ball and re-formed into two words: LUCRETIA KING.

'You want me to – you want me to take her soul, myself? Already?'

'It's got to be the first time some time. Do as I do.'

'Who's this?' said Lucretia, curling her lip in disgust.

'My apprentice,' said Death.

'Ha!' Constantia crowed. 'You're getting the apprentice! I'm getting the master, and you're getting the serving boy.'

Death deftly reached over to Constantia and whisked out her soul, the same shade of pink as her bloodstained dress. 'So annoying,' he muttered under his breath.

'Unacceptable!' said Lucretia. 'Get away from me, boy.'

'Go ahead and get it done,' said Death, ignoring her.

'But I can't! I'm human. I mean, if humans *could* pull each other's souls out, it'd happen by accident all the time.'

'It's loose now; she's ready to go.'

'What if a doctor could . . . ?'

'It's her time. No one can put her back together now. Not all the king's horses and all the king's men. Would you rather leave her to suffer?'

Lucretia huffed. 'I'm waiting!'

Valentine reached out and willed his hand not to shake. He could do this. He had to.

There, not an inch above her face, the air had a different texture. It was subtle, but he could feel it. Her soul, a little loose from her body. He dug his fingertips in and drew his hand back. There was a tug, a fraction of weight and resistance, like fabric snagged on a nail and then—'I've got it!'

Lucretia fell quiet. Or at least, her body did. The soul, sparky and wriggly in Valentine's grasp, strained towards the other soul in Death's arms. It gave off a noise like a low growl and strained to get away. The soul Death was holding pushed back towards them. They were like two dogs on the leash, pulling towards each other to fight.

'We'll have to keep these two apart,' said Death. He tucked the soul into a deep pocket in his cloak, and Valentine did likewise.

Death put his fingers in his mouth and whistled. While they waited for Gytrash to thunder into view, Death tugged Valentine's hair playfully. 'Good job, little buddy. Proud of you.'

Valentine turned his head away and smiled. He liked to

hear that he was doing his job well – even if it wasn't the job he would have chosen. He patted the wriggly soul in his pocket to soothe it, marvelling at how normal it seemed now to hold the entire essence of a person in his hands.

Everything had changed. Up until now, he had followed Death like his shadow, observing and absorbing and waiting. But today he had actually taken a soul.

Perhaps, he considered as Gytrash's echoing hoofbeats drew closer, deep down he'd expected that this apprenticeship would be stopped. The hospital governors would arrive to claim him and insist that he be sent to the watchmaker after all. Or Death would realize that caring for a living human was a lot of work and drop him back at the hospital gates. Or just maybe, he'd open his eyes one morning and find himself back in the dormitory, the last month nothing more than an incredibly vivid dream.

Those thoughts were gone. The moment he removed Lucretia King's soul from her body, he had become a reaper.

And it wasn't so bad, after all.

Journeyed Beyond the Veil

All the way home, the soul of Lucretia King squirmed and writhed, trembling with fury. Valentine felt like he was trying to carry a sack full of angry vipers, all twisting and waiting for a chance to bite.

'We had best take these two straight across,' said Death as they dismounted.

'Across where?' said Valentine, his hair blowing over his eyes from the gust of wind as Gytrash departed.

'Across the void,' said Death.

'Void?'

'Beyond the veil. The great hereafter. You know . . .'

Valentine didn't know.

Inside the mausoleum, Captain Bones was snoring, curled up in one of the coffin niches. Atropos was perched above, her sharp and sinister eyes glinting through the gloom.

Death stooped down and lifted a stone floor slab as though it weighed nothing at all. There were steps beneath it, descending into the earth below the graveyard.

Captain Bones, roused by the noise, trotted over curiously. He took one look down the hole and immediately turned and retreated to his spot. Valentine didn't blame him.

'We're going down here,' said Death, already a few steps down.

'Do I have to?'

At this, Atropos stretched her wings and swooped over to Valentine's shoulder. She tugged his collar with her sharp beak in a *do as you're told* sort of way.

'Fine, I'm going.'

Stacked up on the top few steps were the souls they had collected over the last four days, glowing gently.

'I usually take them down in batches,' said Death, scooping them up. He handed two more to Valentine, and kept hold of the rest, tucking them into various pockets and holding the last few in his arms. 'It saves time.'

The steps went down much further than Valentine had expected. There were no handrails, and at either side was the blackest type of emptiness, like a bottomless well. Valentine's knees were shaky, like he might forget how to walk straight and plunge off the edge. He tried not to think about it.

A hazy pinkish glow awaited them at the bottom and there was a faint strain of music. It was familiar, though Valentine couldn't identify it, and when he tried to concentrate on it, it faded away altogether, only returning when his mind was elsewhere. It was calming, and the soul in his pocket finally began to still itself.

With a defiant squawk, Atropos left Valentine's shoulder and flew back up towards the mausoleum.

After what might have been three minutes or thirty, they reached a large but plain wooden door, and in front of it, a doormat which said PLEASE WIPE YOUR FEET.

'Stay close to me, Valentine,' said Death. 'This place is not meant for living people, and I don't want you getting any strange ideas.'

The door opened and Death stepped through. Valentine wiped his feet and then followed.

'Whoa. Where are we?'

They were in a vast octagonal room with ceilings even higher than a cathedral's, and brightly lit, even though Valentine could see no lamps or candles, and no windows. Where could the light be coming from, this far underground?

Each of the eight walls had a door in the centre, and between and around and above each door were rows and rows and rows of bookshelves.

The Foundling Hospital had a sizeable library donated by its benefactors, with hundreds and hundreds of books – mostly serious and sensible works about philosophy and mathematics. But it could have fitted in this room a thousand times over and still not filled all the shelves. How could anyone in the world afford so many books?

'Put the souls down on the floor, Valentine.' Death set a skeletal hand heavily on his shoulder. 'And don't forget the one in your pocket.'

Valentine did so, his gaze still travelling along the walkways, up and down the spiral staircases, into the myriad alcoves.

'Heavens, Connie, isn't this something?'

Valentine turned sharply at this unexpected voice. Without him noticing, the soul he'd placed down had reformed itself into the shape of Lucretia King, uninjured and free from bloodstains, if a little more transparent than before.

He turned full circle and, sure enough, Constantia had done the same thing.

Already halfway up the nearest set of stairs was the woman who'd asked him to put her wig on. And Gideon Pike was coming closer to them, almost unrecognizable now that he wasn't thin and sunken.

Lucretia linked arms with her cousin, and they wandered off together the best of friends.

'They fought to the death,' said Valentine.

'And yet they can't keep away from each other.'

'Thank you, sir,' said Gideon to Death. His hand reached up to doff his hat before he realized he didn't have one, so he settled instead for a small bow.

'Come with me.' A figure beckoned to Gideon from an alcove. 'I know what it is you seek.'

The figure – he? She? – was different from the re-formed souls. Dressed in a simple sandy-coloured robe, they wore a serene expression. Valentine was sure he recognized them, but as soon as he looked away, he couldn't remember the face at all.

'Who are they?' said Valentine. There were more of these robed figures, wandering the lengths of the shelves, taking a book down here and replacing one there. 'Are they angels? Or librarians?'

'What's the difference?' said Death.

The Library

The library is an in-between space, a resting point on the journey from here to the hereafter.

For every person there is a book. It holds answers to the questions your soul has been asking all your life. When the book – and the life – is finished, it will be waiting in the library.

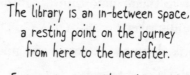

'Explore,' said Death. 'But don't go through any doors, whatever you do.'

'Why? Where do they go?'

'Seven of the eight lead to different crossing points, all over the globe. Best not to pop out in Bhutan and get lost.'

'Oh, right.' Valentine nodded. The doors all looked similar – sturdy wood with shiny brass handles. He made a point of staring at the door they had entered through, noting its position, the wear of the wood, the exact shape of the handle – it would be too easy to forget which one was theirs. 'And the eighth?'

'I'll show you when it is time. It's worth the wait.'

Every book was different: size and shape and colour; some very decorative, and others very plain. Most were not written in English – some not even in any alphabet Valentine knew – but in all cases there was a name on the front in gold ink. He lifted down a dusty volume bound in blue leather and opened it at random.

Miles walked: 52,606.
Steps taken: 110,946,054.
Boots worn out: 27 pairs.

He flipped to another page. This one had a heading 'Lost Things'.

First milk tooth, 17 June 1712, dropped through gap in floorboards.
Left glove, 1 November 1712, fell out of pocket during church.
Self-confidence, 19 March 1714, shamed by Sunday school teacher for struggling to write.

Valentine was fascinated. All these tiny moments, all these insignificant happenings in the life of an ordinary person, all recorded. A few pages later, he found a dense list of every time somebody had had nice thoughts about that person.

30 September 1724: Peggy Swan wishes you would ask her to dance.

1 October 1724: Father thinks how proud he is to see you learning your trade.

2 October 1724: Mother fondly remembers you learning to tie your own bootlaces.

He snapped the book closed, overcome with jealousy. If Valentine ever got to read his own book, this page would be very different. No one would remember when he'd learned to tie his laces. No parent would be proud of him for learning a trade. The Foundling Hospital didn't even get his apprenticeship papers right.

The book became unbearably heavy in his arms. He had always felt alone. Cared for, but not cared about. The only ones who would even notice when he was gone were a stray dog he found in a graveyard, and the physical manifestation of Death. And Philomena, he hoped.

He mustn't be ungrateful. This was his lot in life, and he'd best be thankful for it. Shoving the book back on to the shelf, he stuck out his chin and turned away. Death was right behind him, and Valentine felt embarrassed and guilty, as though Death might know what he was thinking.

'Something's about to happen,' said Death ominously. 'Come and see.'

In the centre of the room, Gideon Pike stood facing one of the doors.

'This must be the eighth door, the odd one out,' whispered Valentine as they approached. Confirming his suspicion, this door had something carved into the wood which he hadn't seen from across the room – the number eight, lying on its back. 'Why did they carve the eight sideways?'

'It's not an eight,' said Death.

'I'm ready,' Gideon said to Death.

'You can go through whenever you wish,' said Death. 'There's no rush. Did you find all your answers?'

Gideon nodded. 'They loved me. They knew that I loved them. What else could I ever need to know?'

That heartsick pang tugged at Valentine again, but he tried to ignore it. There was another sensation too: the tiny hairs on his arms began to stand on end in anticipation . . . though of what, he didn't know.

'Shall we, then?' said Death.

Gideon Pike walked to the eighth door and swung it open confidently. Death shepherded Valentine after him, firmly taking hold of the boy's collar.

'Just in case,' he said in response to Valentine's quizzical look. 'Don't get too close. I don't want your soul sucked from your body prematurely.'

'My . . . what?!'

But they were already through the door.

If the library was impressive, this room was nothing short of miraculous.

They were in an enormous cave carved from glittering rock. In the centre was a vast column of swirling, foaming,

93

misty light, which seemed to stretch from deep below ground right up through the roof. Every colour of the rainbow, and some Valentine had never seen before, teemed within it. Pops and flashes and ribbons of light chased each other, weaving in and out, taking shape for an instant before dissolving back into the whole like a breaking wave.

Now he understood why Death was holding on to his collar. He grabbed hold of Death's cloak too, just to be sure, because he could feel it calling to him. It wanted him to go to it.

Gideon Pike approached the swirling colours, back straight, chin high, bathed in light.

'What's happening?' whispered Valentine.

'He's going back into the Always.'

'The Always,' Valentine murmured. 'Back?'

'It's where you go, between lifetimes,' said Death. 'The souls go back into the Always. They mix together there until they're ready for another life. Then they emerge somewhere else in time and space and do it all over again.'

'What does it feel like, the Always?' said Valentine.

'I don't know,' said Death. 'I can't go any further than this.'

Valentine didn't need an answer anyway. Although his brain didn't quite understand, his soul hummed and fluttered inside his body – it recognized this place.

At that moment the soul that used to be Gideon Pike stepped forward and the Always embraced him, his human shape dissolving into a beautiful shimmer of purple and floating gracefully into the mix. And Valentine knew there was only comfort there. Only light and warmth and companionship and rest.

'Time to go,' said Death.

'I want to stay a little longer,' Valentine protested.

'I know,' said Death. 'And that's why we have to go. You shouldn't be down here too long.'

'It's beautiful.'

'So is the world, Valentine Crow. This will still be here for you when your day comes.'

He swept them away, and Valentine gave a last, longing glance towards the Always as the door closed behind them.

'That was . . . That was . . .' Valentine struggled to find the words as they trudged back up the stairs to the mausoleum. 'I thought there would be answers, but I just have more questions.'

'Yes. The world is like that, sometimes.' Death snapped his fingers and the stone slab scraped its way back into the hole, sealing the entrance to the library below. 'Let's get some fresh air.'

They emerged into the open and Valentine was disoriented to realize it was still morning, crisp and bright and chilly. It was as though they had been underground for a hundred years. A fine, powdery dust had settled over their clothes, which sparkled as it caught the sunlight.

'What's this?' said Valentine, brushing it from his shoulders.

'Time,' said Death. 'Gets everywhere. Never washes out, either. You think you've got rid of it all and you're still finding bits of it in your eye sockets weeks later.' He pinched the front of his cloak and shook it out, a fine cloud diffusing into the air around him. 'It also makes a lovely soup.'

Valentine wasn't sure if that was a joke. While Death was busy stamping the powder out from between his toe bones, Valentine swiped a finger across his dusty sleeve and tentatively put it to his tongue. It crackled and tingled, and, for a moment, tasted exactly like the year 1541.

'So now you know,' said Death. 'The Always. Quite something, isn't it?'

Valentine sat down on the grass and pulled his knees up, trying to make sense of the turmoil inside him.

On one hand, it was comforting to know that the souls they were reaping were going to a good place. He was probably the only living person to know about the Always. It wasn't scary, after all. On the other hand, visiting the library had stirred something deep inside his belly. Something he was usually better at ignoring. A fierce, gnawing loneliness.

Captain Bones stopped rolling in the dirt and came over to lie down on the edge of Valentine's cloak.

'Why so silent, Valentine?' said Death after a while.

'I was thinking about what Gideon Pike said. That people loved him and that's all that mattered.'

'But why does that make you sad?'

'No one ever loved me.'

'That isn't true,' said Death.

Valentine plucked a grass stalk and ran it through his fingers, watching the feather-soft seeds fall away.

'At the Foundling Hospital, we used to imagine who our parents might be. We'd say, bet I have seven brothers. Bet my father's made his fortune at sea. Bet my mother was a countess and she'll take me to live in her castle.' He blew the remaining seeds from his palm. 'I'd have been happy with anyone. Street sweeper would've been good enough for me. Just knowing that somebody wanted me.'

'Somebody does,' said Death. 'Someone out there is looking for you, just like you're looking for them.'

'Who, then?' said Valentine, tugging at his bootlace.

'I don't know. But you'll know them when you find them. Your souls will recognize each other – kindred spirits.'

'What d'you mean?'

Death settled himself down on the edge of a raised slab, his cadaverous toes poking out from the bottom of his cloak. 'There will be some that you spend years with. Some you might only have for a little while. That's all right. Your paths will cross again.'

'One would be enough,' said Valentine, under his breath.

'Come on, Valentine. You're bringing the mood down. That's usually my job.'

Kindred Spirits

The earth travels around the sun, and the moon around the earth. Each one follows their own path, but they are held together by invisible bonds.

Souls are connected in the same way. Certain souls belong together. Again and again, their lifetimes overlap. They are born close to each other, but in a different pattern each time, shuffled up like a deck of cards.

A brother in this life might have
been a friend in the last,
and might be a daughter
in the next.

A cosmic family.

They call to each other through time, and if
they are born far apart, they spend their
lives searching for one another.

That's why people fall in love at first sight,
and why sometimes, when you make a new
friend, it feels like you've
known them for ever.

You've
already
loved them
in another
life

Cut Down in His Prime

Over the next week or so, Valentine practised reading his watch, and with Death's encouragement, he led them across London one collection at a time.

Valentine felt a shiver of unease every time he reached out to take a soul. He reminded himself that these souls were headed to the calm library and the glowing welcome of the Always. He repeated Death's words in his mind – that they were not causing the lives to end, simply helping them to move on. And when those things weren't enough, he focused solely on being a good apprentice. He had a job to do, and that was that.

Besides, they were so busy he didn't have the time or energy to think much about what they were doing. For every soul that showed up on Valentine's apprentice pocket watch,

Death's watch had ten. He kept hoping for an excuse to slip away and visit Philomena, but he barely had time to eat and sleep after his work was done.

After the scolding from his visitor about feeding Valentine properly, Death had begun bringing back various food items he'd collected while Valentine slept. On this morning, Valentine had been woken and presented with an unusual but satisfying breakfast of blackberry jam on crackers and a large raw carrot, laid out on a tree stump. Death looked extremely proud, and Bones looked very hopeful that some scraps would come his way.

Atropos swooped into view, landing gracefully on a headstone close to Death's hand. In her beak was a neat rectangle of paper.

Death accepted it. 'I wasn't expecting a letter.'

The paper had a thick black border, like a funeral invitation. Death unfolded it.

Atropos stuck her chest out and cawed at the dog, as if reminding him that *she* was more useful.

Bones made a half-snarl and turned his back on the bird.

'Oh dear,' Death muttered. 'Surely not.'

Valentine didn't want to pry into Death's private

correspondence, so he pretended not to notice.

Atropos hopped off the edge of the gravestone and dropped noiselessly to the ground behind Captain Bones, who was lying down, his head resting on his front paws in readiness for a good doze, his tail softly twitching from side to side.

'. . . the last thing we need . . .' Death continued.

Valentine stole a peep from the corner of his eye – Death was rubbing his forehead with his knuckle bones.

Atropos hopped forward once, twice, three times, lowered her head and opened her vicious beak.

'Don't you dare,' whispered Valentine to the malevolent bird.

'This is a disaster,' mumbled Death.

In one swift movement, the crow gave the dog's tail a sharp tug and took off out of reach as Bones jerked to his feet. He barked furiously in her direction while she settled smugly in the branches of a nearby yew tree and made a cackling noise that had to be laughter.

'Rude,' scolded Valentine, but the bird didn't care. She flew over to Death's shoulder as he finished reading his letter. Bones clambered on to Valentine's lap and barked defiantly at Atropos again.

Death took a few steps out into the graveyard, then shaded his eye sockets with his hand, peering in all directions. '. . . No reason she'd be here,' he muttered under his breath. 'It's all secure. And she wouldn't know where to look . . .'

'Excuse me,' said Valentine, after a few more seconds of

Death's restless pacing. 'Is something the matter?'

'I'm afraid so,' said Death. 'Brace yourself. You might want to sit down.'

'I am sitting down,' said Valentine.

'She's back. The worst person in the universe. Ohhhh, she's a sly one. I knew she'd find an excuse to come after me.'

Cold uneasiness spread through the air. If Death was worried, that probably meant Valentine ought to be worried too.

'Who's back?'

'Linda.' He looked straight at Valentine as he said the name, and then went silent, as though Valentine should know the significance.

'Who?'

'She's unspeakably horrible . . .' He sat on a gravestone, then changed his mind and got back off again. 'She's all the bad things you can think of, rolled into one. If she's back, I'm in trouble.'

'Worse than Death?' said Valentine. 'I mean . . . no offence . . .'

'Much worse,' said Death. He shuddered and his bones clanked and rattled together like wooden blocks. 'If you took all the nastiest parts of all the nastiest people in London and boiled them up in a pot until they thickened and concentrated into a syrup, and then mixed that syrup with powdered hatred and baked it in the flames of pure spite, then fed it to a pack of rats, what came out the other end would not be half as terrible as her.'

'And you said her name was . . . Linda?' said Valentine.

'That's right,' said Death. 'What's wrong with that?'

'Nothing,' said Valentine. 'Except . . . it's not a very fearsome name, is it?'

'Maybe not to you,' Death answered. 'It strikes fear into my heart every time.'

Atropos cawed in agreement.

'Do you have a heart?' said Valentine.

'Metaphorically speaking,' said Death.

'What is she? Some sort of monster? A demon?'

'Worse,' said Death. 'She's my boss.'

'Huh?'

He waved the black-bordered note in his bony fingers. 'She's going to stick her nose in everywhere and try to find any tiny excuse to get me in trouble. I have to get things in order. You'll be all right here, won't you?'

'Alone?' said Valentine.

'Oh, don't worry, she won't be looking for you.' Death took out his watch and quickly studied it. 'She can't get in here, anyway. You've got the only key. I'm sorry to rush off, but I've got a busy night of collections ahead, so I need to go now, while it's quiet. Don't wander off. Don't talk to any strangers or . . . What's the other thing humans always say to children? Ah. Don't run with scissors. Sit tight.'

'Wait,' said Valentine. A peculiar little shaking sensation came from his pocket. It was his watch, vibrating slightly as though a bee was buzzing about inside it. It seemed as if the watch was reminding him to check it. He clicked open the case, and sure enough. 'Look. I've got a collection due, too.' One week, one day, one hour . . . 'It's already past the hour mark.'

Death leaned over to look. 'So it is. I'm afraid you'll have to take care of that one alone, little brother. You know what to do.'

'I can't! What if I don't find them?'

'You can. Follow the watch.'

'But—'

Death held up one finger. He placed his watch alongside Valentine's for a long moment.

'It's local.' He snapped his watch closed. 'Do you remember your way back to the gate? The one to get to the market?'

Valentine nodded. He wasn't an idiot.

'Head through there. Then let the watch point the way.' Death patted him on the shoulder. 'Chin up, Valentine, there's a good lad. Don't be late. And remember to lock the gate behind you!' And with a gust of air and a rasping of wings, Valentine's master was gone.

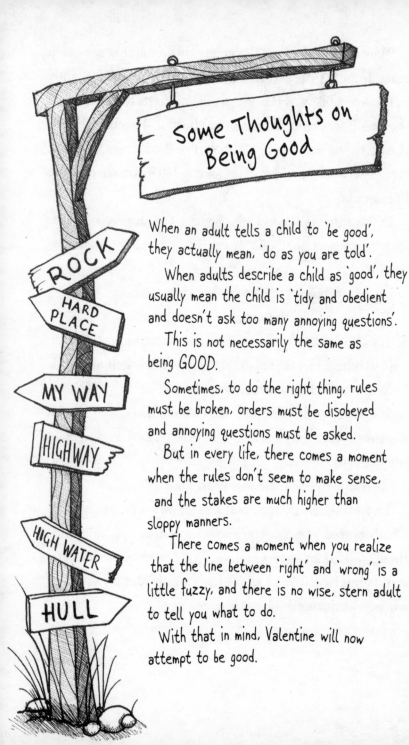

Some Thoughts on Being Good

ROCK

HARD PLACE

MY WAY

HIGHWAY

HIGH WATER

HULL

When an adult tells a child to 'be good', they actually mean, 'do as you are told'.

When adults describe a child as 'good', they usually mean the child is 'tidy and obedient and doesn't ask too many annoying questions'.

This is not necessarily the same as being GOOD.

Sometimes, to do the right thing, rules must be broken, orders must be disobeyed and annoying questions must be asked.

But in every life, there comes a moment when the rules don't seem to make sense, and the stakes are much higher than sloppy manners.

There comes a moment when you realize that the line between 'right' and 'wrong' is a little fuzzy, and there is no wise, stern adult to tell you what to do.

With that in mind, Valentine will now attempt to be good.

Returned to the Earth

Valentine stared, disbelieving, into the empty space where Death used to be.

He had been an apprentice for less than six weeks, and now he had to venture out *all by himself* and take a soul.

'Is Linda really that bad?' he asked Atropos.

The bird bowed her head gravely.

'Oh dear.'

He checked the pocket watch. It wasn't quite halfway through the hour section, but not far off, either. He could do this. He had the cloak, and the watch. He'd taken a soul before and used the compass to find his way. The only difference now was that Death wasn't there to sort it out if things went awry.

'I'll leave now,' he announced out loud. 'Better to be early than late.'

Thus resolved, he left the mausoleum and marched through the graveyard, acting out a confidence he didn't feel. Atropos came too, flying a few gravestones ahead, then letting him catch up. No doubt she was coming to keep her beady eye on him, rather than to encourage him, but Valentine was glad of her company anyway. Bones lolloped along behind them, tongue hanging out, just eager to be part of the team.

Valentine unlocked the gate and peered through. Nobody was watching, so he stepped out and waited for Atropos to fly through behind him.

'Bones, you'd better stay here.'

The dog yapped an objection and growled at Atropos.

'Sorry, boy,' said Valentine. 'Death said I can't take you on collections. We won't be long.'

Atropos watched from the top of the railings as he locked the gate, then hopped down on to Valentine's shoulder, for once not digging her claws in uncomfortably hard. He wished the other Foundlings could see him with a giant tame crow – they'd be so jealous.

But he had work to do.

He opened his watch and tapped the glass. As before, the particles of gold rose up through the liquid, which began to swirl and spiral until the golden dust had wrapped itself into the tiny star. Valentine tried to slow his breathing and steady his hands, making himself as still and calm as he could manage. He focused all of his attention on the watch, trying to notice everything about it, every movement and sensation and every tick of the hands edging closer to their inevitable destination.

The star shape bobbed, then drifted across. Valentine turned his whole body to face that direction. And then he felt the *pull*, like the watch was telling him that he was right. *Head this way.*

He felt a flicker of pleasure. He continued straight in that direction. Although Valentine ought to stand out with a long black cloak and huge black bird on his shoulder, nobody was looking at them.

He stared intently at the watch, adjusting his direction to line himself up with the star. The soul's hand, this one a brassy yellow with a single diamond shape cut out, edged ever closer to the next mark.

Then something caught his foot, and he stumbled on a missing cobble. He staggered forward and almost regained his balance, until his other foot stepped on the end of his too-long cloak and down he came. Instinctively he held the watch in close to his chest. Atropos landed gracefully on the ground beside him and cawed at him aggressively.

'I didn't do it on purpose!' He straightened himself up. One advantage of being unnoticed was that no one saw him trip.

As he followed the path of the watch, he had to divert round a number of buildings, plus a cart selling apples and an open coal-hole. Each time, he grew a little bit more anxious, worried that he'd lose his way, or be delayed. Something was changing, though. The watch was behaving differently. It was very subtle, but it seemed to be pulling harder, and it quaked a little in his grip.

'We must be close,' he whispered to Atropos. The star urged him to turn the next corner. Partridge Street. He knew that name. Why did he know that name? He had never been to this part of London before.

There was a tavern and a jumble of small shops and houses, all competing for space, and plenty of people around. A barber shop with a red-and-white pole outside sat between a pawnbroker and a house with the word Dog painted ominously on the door.

A sign outside the corner house was painted, rather badly, in garish colours. A beer jug. A pestle and mortar. And a woman holding a piglet. No. A *baby*.

This was the midwife's house. Partridge Street! That's

where Philomena said her new mistress was.

He looked back at the watch, hoping it was leading him to another house, but it pointed insistently at this one. He approached slowly. Poor Philomena. If her mistress died, she'd have to go back to the Foundling Hospital until they found her another apprenticeship. That'd be terrible luck for her. Terrible luck for him, too, since she might end up much further away, where they wouldn't see each other.

Or – a horrible thought – what if a newborn was about to share the same fate as so many workhouse babies. Valentine shuddered.

Then again, Valentine hadn't thought to ask who else lived in the house. Maybe there was some old, ailing grandparent living there. Or perhaps the midwife was nursing someone who was sick.

He tapped the glass, dreading to see what name would be called forth.

The star dissolved and the gold rearranged itself painfully slowly into words.

'No!' he gasped, but plain as day it read:

Kicked the Bucket

Of all the people in London, the watch had led him to the one person he'd call a friend. Philomena. Valentine knew that young people did sometimes die and that no one was really safe when cholera swept through the city. But there was something hideous about somebody his own age dying.

'Atropos, I know this girl,' he said quietly. 'I don't think I can do it.'

Atropos tugged sharply on his ear. The hand had now entered the five-minutes section of the watch. Reluctantly Valentine walked forward. A note propped up inside the window showed a large black arrow pointing to the rear of the house.

It was the end of a crooked row of squat but sturdy

buildings, slightly bigger than its neighbours. Where the back of the house ended, the wall continued at head height enclosing a small yard, and stretching out and over the roadway were the branches of a thick and hardy old pear tree. Valentine reached a roughly made wooden gate. The sound of humming came from beyond it – he recognized the tune as one they'd often sung in the Foundling chapel.

There was a gap in the wood big enough to peer through and he pressed his face to it. There was Philomena, hanging up shirts and smocks on a clothesline, cheerful and healthy.

It wasn't sickness, then. She hadn't been struck down with some terrible, incurable fever, and it didn't appear that she was hurt or injured in any way. Her death must be a dreadful accident, then – something sudden and unexpected.

A tingling sensation began at the base of Valentine's spine.

Atropos was evidently sick of waiting. She flew to the top of the wall, glared briefly back at him, then swooped down into the yard.

Valentine knocked on the gate.

'If you're dropping off mending, come straight in,' shouted Philomena. 'My hands are full.'

After one last glance at his watch – two, maybe three minutes to go – Valentine opened the gate, with anxious, sweaty hands.

'Philomena, it's me,' he said.

'Valentine!' her face was hidden by the apron she was pinning out, but she sounded happy that he was there, which made him feel even worse. 'I was worried you wouldn't come.'

'Me too,' he said. 'Is anything wrong?'

'Wrong?' Her head popped round the side of a sheet. 'Why would anything be wrong?'

'I don't know,' he said. 'You're not hurt, or anything?'

'You're an odd duck, Valentine.' She went through the open back door into the kitchen of the house. He trailed behind her, alert for anything amiss. No candles threatening to catch her dress on fire; no heavy objects balanced precariously on high shelves; no open trapdoor into a dark, foreboding cellar beneath.

She snatched up a large basket full of folded linen. 'Another drop-off. You can come with me if you want – it isn't far.' They silently crossed the yard and stepped out into the street.

Even though it was tucked safely in his pocket, Valentine could picture the watch hand ticking closer and closer to Philomena's appointed end. If he saw it coming, should he prevent whatever tragedy was about to befall her? Was it even possible? Outside the tavern two men were unloading enormous flour sacks from a cart while a boy held on to the horse. Two rather rough-looking chaps were having an animated conversation about a dogfight on the other side of the street. Several women, one flanked by two small children, carried baskets on their way back from the market.

'Are you going to tell me what your trade is yet?' Philomena asked.

'Umm . . .' He was saved by Atropos, who chose that moment to catch up with them, landing right on the top of his head. Her scratchy claws didn't hurt him, but it felt like they could if she wanted them to.

'Wigs and whiskers!' Philomena stopped mid-crossing. 'Valentine! A huge black bird just landed on your head!'

He laughed. 'This is Atropos. Say hello, girl.' He used his most encouraging voice. The bird hopped down on to his right shoulder and gave him a scornful sideways glare.

'She's gorgeous,' said Philomena. 'Is she your pet?'

'She belongs to my master.'

Atropos puffed her chest up and shook her feathers angrily, as if to point out that she belonged to no one but herself.

'I've never seen a tame crow before. Ain't she a beauty?' Philomena tentatively reached out to the bird, who surprisingly allowed her to stroke her wing with the back of her hand.

It happened very fast.

Over by the tavern, a plank of wood fell from the back of a cart and hit the flagstones with an unusually loud crack. The startled horse reared up, yanking the rope out of the boy's hand so fast he could do nothing but cower from its hoofs. It charged away in uncontrollable panic, the cart bouncing and swinging behind it. Philomena barely had time to look over her shoulder before it was there.

But so was Valentine. He lunged forward and shoved her shoulder, knocking Philomena back into the gutter and falling after her. White linens fell gracefully, drifting across the dirty ground. Hoofs clattered inches from Valentine's body as he wrapped his arms over his head. A cartwheel bumped clumsily beside him, then rolled away.

He sat up. Philomena sat up too, face mud-splattered, eyes wide but his body unhurt. Her basket traced a lazy arc on the ground before settling in a dip in the cobbles. Atropos landed on top of it and squawked furiously at Valentine.

'Sorry, Atropos, I didn't have time to think.'

The men ran past after their horse and cart, waving arms and shouting for the beast to stop.

'You saved my life,' said Philomena.

'I had to.'

Valentine got to his feet, shaking dust and general street-muck from the folds of his cloak. He offered a hand to Philomena, who took it gratefully.

'All your laundry is filthy. Will you be in trouble?'

'Probably,' said Philomena. 'Better in trouble than trampled, though.'

Valentine shooed Atropos off the rim of the basket and righted it, and they began gathering up the muddied clothes. Atropos stalked along beside him indignantly, keeping pace with Valentine, not allowing him to look away. He knew what she was trying to tell him, but he ignored her.

'I'd better get straight back to it.' Philomena picked up the basket. 'I'll be working all night trying to get this lot clean. But thank you, Valentine. That could've been really awful.'

Unexpectedly, she put out her free arm and pulled him into a hug. He hugged her back. It felt nice.

Then he felt something else. A catch in the air, a boundary . . . a soul.

Philomena's soul, coming loose from her body. Immediately he dropped his arms to his sides and stepped sharply back from her.

He didn't need to check the watch to know. Her death

time had passed, but she was still alive.

'What's wrong?' said Philomena. 'Are you hurt?'

Valentine shook his head and took another step back. He had witnessed how easily souls could be parted from the flesh once they became loose. If he got too close, he might pull Philomena's soul out by accident.

'Oh . . . should I not have done that?' Philomena backed away awkwardly. 'Sorry. I thought . . . Sorry.'

'No!' said Valentine. She looked embarrassed and hurt, but there was no way he could explain that he was on his way to collect her soul, then decided to save her, and now had to run away in case he accidentally reaped her soul after all. 'No, it wasn't the hug. But I've . . . I have to go. Right away. I remembered something . . . Sorry.'

He ran back the way he came, allowing himself one single glance over his shoulder at Philomena, left dejected in the street. He wondered if he would have to avoid her for ever, or if the soul would heal back into the body in a few days, once the death hour was further away.

But for now, he needed to get out of there.

He strode back towards the cemetery gate. Atropos caught up with him with a few strong wing flaps, and proceeded to caw loudly, right down his ear.

'I know you're angry

with me, but she's fine,' Valentine said stubbornly. 'She's not suffering, and she never was. Death says he's releasing them from the suffering.'

At the gate he took out his key with shaky hands, his emotions rocking wildly from excitement to dread like a ship thrown around in a storm. Bones was still faithfully waiting for him to return, and Valentine scooped the little dog up and hugged him tightly.

He was exhilarated and also rather scared. He had broken a rule. A big one. The very first time Death had sent him out to work on his own. But he had done a good thing. 'I made sure she was never suffering to begin with.'

A good thing indeed.

Faced Judgement

As Valentine walked back through the graveyard, doubt began to set in.

He'd made the right choice; he was sure of it. What monster would stand by and let his friend have a terrible accident? But something gnawed away inside him – he hadn't done his job. When Death asked where the soul was, should he try to cover his tracks or be honest? Valentine couldn't help but dread the consequences.

Too late to question things now. He checked his watch. Philomena's hand was still visible on the dial – it hadn't disappeared when it reached the end, as all the others did. In fact, it seemed to be turning the opposite way, edging back towards the hour section. What could that mean?

He hoped it was a good sign – moving away from her death

time had to be positive, right? Perhaps it would travel all the way round the dial backwards and disappear at the other end.

'Oh, good, you're back,' said Death the moment Valentine unlocked the mausoleum door. 'As soon as you were gone, I thought, maybe this is a bad idea, splitting up.'

Death tapped his bony fingertips together, talking more to himself than Valentine. He lit the candle as Valentine closed the door.

'Were you sitting in the dark?' Valentine asked, but Death's thoughts were elsewhere.

'If *she* sees someone else reaping – well, that's suspicious, isn't it?' He stopped abruptly.

Valentine's breath caught in his throat, certain Death would ask for the soul and find out what he had done.

'You didn't see anyone out there, did you?' Death asked. 'Anyone paying too much attention to you working?'

Valentine shook his head.

'That's good. That would be a disaster.'

'Why would it be a disaster?' asked Valentine.

Death continued, mostly to himself. 'Even if she didn't know you were with me, she probably has a list and knows where every other reaper is supposed to be, and you wouldn't be on it. She's always got a list. Records. Paperwork.' He spat out the last words with absolute disgust.

'Other reapers? Are there more of you?' Valentine asked.

But Death didn't seem to hear his questions, too busy with

his own thoughts. 'Of course, if we stick together, that might draw more attention. Two reapers. Not standard practice. Nope, can't have her seeing you with me.'

'Why not?' said Valentine. 'Why wouldn't your apprentice be by your side? Isn't that the whole point, to learn the trade?' There was something very unsettling about this conversation, although it did mean that Death wasn't asking about Philomena's soul, which was a blessing.

'Ah.' Death cracked his knuckles nervously and gave an apologetic shrug. 'Sit down, Valentine.'

Valentine dragged one of the small wooden crates up to the stone table and sat down. Death did the same on the opposite side, his long, narrow body hunching down to more closely match Valentine's height. His wide, heavy sleeves fell in folds against the stone as he rested his skeletal elbows on the slab.

'Funny story,' said Death. 'The thing is . . . I'm not *technically* allowed an apprentice.'

'Huh?'

Death chuckled awkwardly and adjusted the neckline of his cloak.

'Ah, I'm not, I mean, I *have* had an apprentice before, of course. I know what I'm doing. Of course I do. I've been in this job for a long time. And I mean, a *long* time – you don't even know. Your tiny human brain couldn't even grasp the length of time—'

'But you're not allowed one now?' Valentine interrupted.

'Right. Just a formality. Technically, according to "the rules" –' he made quotation marks in the air – 'only level nines and above are allowed to have an apprentice. Or an assistant. And I'm a level nineteen.'

'Nineteen is higher than nine.'

'Incorrect. The levels go up to thirteen, and then back down again on the other side.'

'Why?'

'Because those are the rules. And the rules say I'm not allowed an apprentice at my level.'

'But you said you've had one before.'

'Yes . . . I used to be a fifteen. I was, um, demoted.'

'What does that mean?'

'It means,' he replied through gritted teeth, 'that I had a better job, and then I got sent back to a worse job.'

'Why?'

'It's a long story.'

'I'm here for seven years . . .'

From some distance away, they heard barking, as though Captain Bones had found something very interesting in the far corner of the graveyard.

Valentine and Death turned their heads towards the mausoleum door.

A pause. More barking. A little louder.

'That's ominous,' said Death.

'I'll check on him,' said Valentine, getting to his feet.

123

Death shook his head and held up his hand to indicate Valentine should stay exactly where he was.

The yapping continued, now interspersed with the odd growl. Death stood up and stuck his head right through the closed wooden door, then withdrew it a moment later.

'Valentine?' said Death. 'When you came back from your collection . . .'

Uh oh, this was it – he had been found out.

'. . . is there any chance you forgot to lock the cemetery gate?'

OMINOUS

om-in-uss

A troubling sign, or warning of looming misfortune.

For example:

A dark cloud warning of a ruined picnic.

Or

The frantic yapping of a graveyard dog warning of an extremely **unwelcome visitor.**

Pushing up Daisies

'Don't panic!' said Death, although it was very clear that he was panicking. 'She must have found her way in through the gate. The graveyard is compromised. Very good. No problem. Nothing to worry about.'

He stuck his head back through the solid door again.

'Don't worry, Valentine,' he muttered. 'She's not after you.'

Valentine didn't really understand what had him terrified. He was Death. Things feared him.

'Right,' said Death. 'This is what we're going to do.' He ushered Valentine out of the way and lifted the giant stone slab in the floor. The strange, soft music of the library below spilled out into the mausoleum. 'Quickly. On to the stairs.'

Valentine nodded. A large glass jar without a lid was balanced on the second step, with the bluish swirl of a soul inside.

'I'll take that down later,' said Death, noticing Valentine's gaze. 'If she's here ages, go down to the library. But do NOT go near the Always, even if a soul goes through. *Especially* if a soul goes through. Understood?'

'Got it.'

Death steered Valentine over to the steps and by the time he was eight steps down, Death had already slammed the stone slab over the hole and plunged him into darkness.

Above him the jarred soul glowed faintly like moonlight in a cloudy sky. Valentine shuffled back up the stairs towards it, half crawling for fear of coming too close to the edges in the darkness. He sat down as close as he could to the opening. He needed to know what Death could possibly be scared of. It was frustrating that he couldn't see Linda, although perhaps that was for the best. Death was pretty scary-looking with his empty eye sockets and giant skeletal frame, although Valentine was getting used to him now. If Linda was more important, she must be even scarier. Idly he picked up the jar of soul and peered into it. It was heavy and warm as though it were full of hot soup.

There was a knock on the wooden door of the mausoleum.

A creak as it opened.

'Linda!' Death's greeting was loaded with cheerful surprise. 'What a pleasure!'

'Good afternoon,' said the woman in a flat, business-like tone.

Valentine set the soul down to give his full attention to eavesdropping.

'I got the letter. I didn't know you would handle this personally, though!'

'Why would you? They don't consult level eighteens on management decisions.'

'Oh, um, it's actually nineteen now,' Death said sheepishly.

'Another demotion? Why am I not surprised?'

Death gave a polite, nervous chuckle.

'I've heard that things have fallen to ruin since I've been gone. Standards slipping, and so forth,' Linda added.

'All in order as far as I know.'

'Which isn't saying much, considering how little you know.'

Wow, thought Valentine.

'Good one,' choked out Death. 'Very witty.'

'You won't mind me checking for myself, then.'

'Of course not,' said Death.

Footsteps over the mausoleum floor. Linda's voice was slightly louder now – she must be standing on the slab right above Valentine's head. 'Is this the portal you're using these days? Show me.' She stamped her heel on the stone.

'Delighted to,' yelped Death, and Valentine shuffled

a few steps further down, torn between listening in and running away. 'But . . . it's not a great time, very busy, lots of collections on today, you know how it is – so, another day. Next week, or actually, how about some time in March?'

'I have a better idea,' said Linda. 'I'll come with you.'

'Ah . . .' said Death. 'Perfect. I can't think of any good reason why that can't happen.' And then, in an even louder voice. 'And when we get back you certainly won't find any souls lying about, waiting to be delivered!'

Valentine got the hint. He picked up the jar and scrambled to his feet.

'Why are you shouting?' said Linda.

'Because I'm so happy to be inspected. Shall we go, then?'

'Yes. Oh, and there's this horrible mangy hound running loose . . .'

Mangy! How dare she insult Captain Bones? Not wanting to hear any more, Valentine began to descend the very long staircase towards the library. With only the dim glow of the soul to guide him, he watched his footing carefully and tried not to think about the black drop at either side of the steps. The soul bubbled and writhed restlessly.

'Don't worry,' said Valentine. 'It's nice in the library; you'll like it.'

The soul made a grumbly sound.

'I think I'm supposed to say your name, but I don't know what it is,' said Valentine apologetically. 'I don't mean to be rude. I'm new at this job.'

He sighed with relief once they were safely at the bottom and opened the door into the library. It was every bit as incredible as the first time he'd seen it. Walls stretched to dizzying heights, uncountable numbers of books occupying every inch, too many to comprehend. Yet it remained cosy and light and peaceful, and smelled like fresh paper and chamomile. The words that came to mind were 'just right'. Everything about the library was just right.

He put the jar down on the floor, waiting for the soul to take form, but nothing happened.

'Out you come, then.'

It didn't. He picked the jar up again.

The soul made another mumbly noise.

'Sorry,' said Valentine. 'I can't understand what you're saying.'

He waited for a few moments, watching the librarians glide from shelf to shelf like honeybees on flowers, hard-working and content. The soul in the jar hadn't budged.

'Are you stuck?' Valentine reached in and attempted to scoop the soul out, but it trickled through his fingers, too watery to be grasped. That explained the jar, then. Setting it down, he walked away and paced restlessly around the library for a few minutes in case it was shy and needed some space. He kept an eye on the jar from a distance, hoping the soul would emerge before Death and Linda arrived at the library.

The minutes ticked slowly by. After waiting for what felt like for ever, Valentine decided he'd had enough. He turned the jar upside down and shook the soul out. It resisted for a moment, then peeled away from the edges of the glass with a slurp and a plop, like jelly from a mould. As it hit the ground it splattered like a raindrop and instantly bounced up into the shape of a man. He looked around, wide-eyed and confused and more than a little angry.

Valentine couldn't exactly remember what he was supposed to say. 'Welcome to being dead.' He'd started all wrong and shook himself. 'Let me explain. This is the library and it's where you – I mean, everyone, not just you—'

'Spit it out, boy,' snapped the man.

'This is where everyone comes after they die. And there's a book—'

'Who are you?' the man interrupted, impatiently. 'I don't talk to children. Where's the big chap with the scary face?'

Valentine stumbled over his words, flustered by this rudeness. 'Death, he's out on another collection. I'm his apprentice.'

'Apprentice! Ha! What sort of slapdash service is this?

I'm going to complain to whoever is in charge. Summon them at once.'

'Um . . .' Valentine shrugged helplessly. 'I don't think there is anyone in charge.'

'You don't think? What is the point of you, then?'

'I'm trying to explain what happens now that you're dead!' Valentine folded his arms defensively.

The man tutted. 'Go ahead, then. Get on with it.'

Valentine took a deep breath and spoke as fast as he could to avoid another interruption. 'There's a book somewhere in here with all the details about your life and you can read it now and find out anything you've been wondering about and then when you're finished you can go through that door over there and your soul will go into the Always again.'

'Which book is mine, then?' He held out his hand. 'Come on, I don't have all day.'

Valentine stared up at the towering bookcases. How on earth were they supposed to find it?

'If he died today,' whispered a voice from beside him, soft and low like a cat's purr, 'his book is by the door you came in through.' It was a librarian. An angel. Whichever. They stood very close to him, and Valentine's frustration at the rude man began to melt away. His breathing became slow and relaxed, his body heavy like in the moments before a deep and delicious sleep. 'Come with me.'

He dreamily followed the librarian towards the door he

had entered through. Once again, as soon as their back was turned, Valentine found himself unable to remember the librarian's face.

'Less disorientating for new arrivals.' They ran their fingers along a shelf stacked with a multitude of books.

'Are you human?' said Valentine.

The librarian smiled.

'I mean, were you human? Once?'

'Am. Was. Could be. Will be.'

Valentine had no idea what this cryptic reply meant.

The librarian lifted down a large biscuit-coloured square book. 'The answer to your other question is in this section too.'

'About you being human?' said Valentine.

'No,' said the librarian. 'The important one.'

'What question?'

The librarian shook their head and put a finger to their lips. 'I'm not supposed to say. It's not your turn yet.'

They glided away, heading towards the impatient soul.

'Stop!' called Valentine, but the librarian did not. 'What important question?'

There was a *clunk-click* in the otherwise near-silent room. The entrance to the library was opening.

'Here we are, then!' Death's voice once again was unnecessarily loud and cheerful. 'Back at the library, like old times.'

Valentine ducked behind the nearest row of bookcases, shielded from the door.

'But listen to me, talking away when you've got so much to do. You must be incredibly busy since the latest promotion. Did I say congratulations, by the way?' From the sound of their voices and footsteps, Valentine could tell they were walking along the other side of the bookcase he was hiding behind. He moved towards the opposite end, ready to dart into the next row if they rounded the corner.

'You did. Twice,' came Linda's monotone voice. It didn't sound like she had cheered up any in the last half an hour or so.

At the end of the row, Valentine poked his head out to get a glimpse of the hideous creature. Death's cadaverous arms were full of souls even though he hadn't been gone for long. He wasn't kidding about a busy afternoon.

'It would be selfish of me to keep you, Linda. I can handle this from here.'

'Why are you trying to get rid of me? Are you hiding something?'

Valentine couldn't see her – she was perfectly blocked by Death's cloak and the end of the bookcase.

He scuttled over to the bottom of a spiral staircase. He grabbed a large blue book with gilded edges and opened it at random, holding it up so that it mostly covered his face as he darted up the stairs. Valentine hoped that if she saw him, he'd be mistaken for another soul in the library.

At the top of the staircase, he stood by a railing and then slowly lowered the book to peer over it. Death's back was towards him, and his giant wings were unfurled, effectively shielding Linda.

Valentine sidled along the railing, keeping the book up, trying to catch a glimpse of her, but just as he did, Death shifted his position so she remained blocked. It was almost as if he was doing it on purpose.

This dance continued for a few minutes more, then Valentine crept downstairs again, falling into step with a passing librarian to shield him from view.

'I'll be watching you very, very closely. And when I find out that you've messed up – when, not if – you'll be bumped right down to level twenty-two.'

Death gasped. 'You wouldn't.'

'Nothing would bring me more pleasure,' said Linda. 'You'll be scraping dead cats off the pavement for the rest of eternity.'

And with that, she was off, striding in his direction. Valentine hastily ducked behind a table. Just as she was passing by, he lifted his head to finally gaze upon the monstrous creature whom Death himself mortally feared.

Dearly Departed

I n the few hours since he had known of her existence, Valentine had painted a mental picture of Linda. Some hideous rotting monster, sharp teeth, pox-ridden grey skin, countless bulging eyeballs. And now she was walking straight past him. And she was . . .

Normal.

Her hair was mousy brown and neatly pinned up. She had the usual number of eyeballs and no obvious fangs.

She crossed the library floor in double-quick time and let herself out through a different doorway than they had entered through. Valentine glanced over at Death just in time to see the cheerful mask fall away and his shoulders slump down.

'That's Linda?' asked Valentine, emerging from his hiding place.

'Yes, that's her. Bone-chilling, isn't she?'

'Is she?' said Valentine.

'Did you see what she was wearing? She's showing off because she's just got back from the twenty-third century.'

'But that's in the future.'

'Future, past, nevermore, for ever, whatever.' He waved dismissively. 'She was assigned there for a stretch and she wants everyone to know it. Big deal. As if I care.' He folded his arms and leaned back against a bookcase with an exaggerated not-bothered pose which suggested he did, in fact, care very much.

''Course you don't,' said Valentine. 'Twenty-third century? Boring.'

'I had the fourteenth century! All of it! By myself! Those were the glory days! I'm telling you, Valentine, a lot of folks were very jealous of that one. Before she had even manifested as solid matter from the cosmic ooze!'

'Cosmic ooze?'

'Don't worry about it. Everything all right? Thanks for moving that soul for me. She's a stickler for those sorts of things.'

He suddenly remembered what the librarian had said. '*The answer to your other question is in this section too.*'

Which question did they mean? He had a hundred of them.

The section nearest the door was the one that held the books of all the newly arrived or almost-due souls. But

Valentine himself wasn't dead or dying, was he?

They passed through the doorway and began their gradual ascent to the surface, Valentine trudging thoughtfully a few steps behind Death, to avoid his colossal wings.

'Mister Death,' he said, when they were halfway up. 'Can I ask you something?'

'You just did.'

'Is there no other place for souls?'

'Other place?'

'I always thought that there'd be a nice place, for the good people. And, for the nasty ones, you know . . .' The soul from the jar had been so unpleasant and demanding, Valentine could only imagine that the man was equally unkind when he was alive.

'Lots of people think that,' said Death. 'The world is unfair, so we imagine it'll all be evened out in the long run. Punishments for those who have wronged you. Et cetera, et cetera. It doesn't work that way.'

'But if no one is keeping score, what's the point? What's the point of being good?'

'Valentine,' said Death, pausing beneath the slab to the mausoleum. 'I'm surprised at you. Surely being good is the point of being good. Being kind. Helping each other. Love.'

Valentine bristled a little bit at this accusation. 'I'm not saying people shouldn't be kind. But it isn't fair. If you can do everything right your whole life while someone else does

138

everything wrong, and then at the end of it all you both get the same treatment.'

Death heaved the stone slab out of the way and climbed out. 'Let's go outside. Some conversations are better held in sunlight.'

Valentine followed him up and out of the mausoleum, and they sat on conveniently sized stones outside. Captain Bones rushed over immediately and tried to clamber into Valentine's lap, his stubby little legs slipping with the effort.

'I should've known that a human apprentice would ask difficult questions. You have to understand, Valentine, that I don't have all the answers. I can tell you what happens. I can't tell you *why* things happen. Some mysteries are beyond even me.'

'It doesn't seem fair,' he repeated, quietly. He scooped Captain Bones into his lap and the dog gave his cheek a big, wet lick, before jumping down again.

'That's one way of looking at it. But on the other hand, is it fair to punish people for every mistake they make? Most people are trying their best, you know. It's a hard world out there.'

'But it's hard for everyone,' Valentine protested. 'And if some people still manage to be good, then there are no excuses for people who don't.'

'Not excuses,' said Death. 'But reasons.' He sighed and stretched. Captain Bones took this as an invitation to play, and hopped over Death's feet, tail wagging. 'But I think . . .

139

Never mind. I shouldn't be saying this. Good and evil. The meaning of life. Way above my level.'

'Please carry on,' said Valentine. 'Please?'

'I think it's about learning. Not getting it right. But trying. And pushing yourself to be better every time. It's like an artist sketching then layering up the paint bit by bit, making mistakes, going over them, making the painting better, selling it for a lot of money, spending the money on more paint, dying before you can use it . . .'

'Huh?'

'Sorry. I picked up the soul of an artist this afternoon. He didn't half make a fuss about wasted paint. My point is, lives aren't finished artworks ready to be hung on the wall and judged. They're messy and complicated and time always runs out before they're finished. But as long as you're trying, you're doing fine. That's what gets you into the Always. And next time you come back, you can try to learn the things you didn't learn this time. Oh no, stop – it tickles!'

Valentine looked up in surprise as Death giggled. Captain Bones was attempting to pull one of Death's toe bones loose.

'No! Bad dog!' Valentine scolded.

Captain Bones let go with a whimper, tucking his tail between his legs. He waddled a few steps away and deliberately turned his back on

Valentine to sulk.

'What about the people who don't try, though?' said Valentine.

'There are fewer of those than you might think.'

'There are *some*, though? What happens to them? What happens to the people who are really, really, really bad? I don't want my soul to be all mixed up in a big soup with horrible, awful people.'

'I was hoping this wouldn't come up for a long time. What with you being human . . . There is somewhere else, for those souls. Or not so much *somewhere* as *nowhere*.'

'Is there or isn't there? I don't understand.'

'There is. But it's not a place. It's more of an absence of a place. The opposite of the Always. The Never.'

Valentine shivered; a sudden, uncontrollable shudder raced up his spine.

'Where is it?'

'Not really anywhere. You don't go to the Never. The Never comes to you.'

Death jumped up.

'Grab your things, Valentine. We're moving house.'

In Eternal Slumber

'Moving house?' asked Valentine.

'The mausoleum is compromised, now,' said Death, 'because *somebody* left the cemetery gate unlocked.'

'Oh . . . yeah,' said Valentine. He had forgotten for a moment that it was his fault Linda had found her way into the graveyard. 'But she probably would've found you somewhere else, eventually.'

Death stared at him, silently. Valentine suspected that if he had eyebrows, they would've been raised.

'Sorry.'

'It's not about her finding me – I can't have her finding *you*. Let's move you in case she makes another unscheduled visit. Have you got your belongings?'

Valentine ducked inside the mausoleum. He turned one of the wooden crates upside down and put the food inside, then blew out the candle, which didn't seem to have burned down at all since they'd first arrived. He dropped that into the crate, too. As he was leaving, he noticed something papery crumpled amongst dry leaves that had blown in from the graveyard. He picked it up and opened it. His apprenticeship papers. He smoothed them out, folded them into neat quarters and shoved them deep into his cloak pocket next to his watch.

'I'm ready,' he said. 'Come on, Bones.'

They had travelled nearly halfway across the graveyard and reached another enormous tomb, which was conveniently screened from both the gate and the mausoleum by three gnarled yew trees. Captain Bones stopped at Valentine's feet, a little out of breath from trotting behind them. Atropos swooped to perch on a low-hanging branch of the nearest yew tree.

This monument was grander than all the others. On either side of the doorway were pillars, exquisitely carved in the shape of women in long flowing robes and veils.

Valentine paused to touch one. It was masterfully made – solid rock sculpted to look like the lightest silk that could be ruffled by the slightest breeze.

'Impressive, isn't it?' said Death. 'An upgrade, really. Wait until you see the inside.' He strode right through the closed door. Valentine, hands still full, fumbled for his key to follow him, and ushered the dog inside.

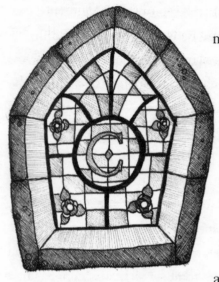

It was nicer than the mausoleum. For one thing, it had windows. Two small stained-glass windows were set into the wall opposite the entrance, casting a pool of light on the stone floor, illuminating the specks of ancient dust disturbed by their arrival. There were no coffin niches here, but below the windows was the most elaborate funeral statue Valentine had ever seen, even within Death's enormous graveyard.

Raised up on a platform at Valentine's head-height was a life-size statue of a man in armour, lying on his side with his head propped up on his left hand. Not the most comfortable position in which to spend eternity. His helmet lay by his elbow, revealing an impressive head of curly hair. In front of him was a statue of a woman in the same position, wearing an enormous ruff. Her gown, carved with the same delicate touch as the columns outside, was covered in a complicated pattern of lace and beads. Both statues were brightly painted in contrast with the grey tones of the cemetery. And both people looked thoroughly bored

144

after two hundred years or so lying in the monument.

'May I introduce Lord and Lady Clench,' said Death.

Valentine put the crate down on the otherwise empty floor and took in the marble walls and paving, as cold and hard as the last place.

Death added, 'I'll get you a mattress. I promise. I forgot that humans are basically a bag of soft bits wrapped in easily bruisable skin.'

Valentine opened his mouth to object but realized that Death was right.

'And we can drag in some extra boxes for chairs. Be cosy, don't you think?'

'Right,' said Valentine. In an effort to look enthusiastic, he walked the perimeter of the room admiring the decorative carvings on the ceiling. 'We can put the candle here.' He grabbed it from the box and balanced it on the edge of Lady Clench's platform. 'And there's a gap here between the statue and the wall. I can put my food here to keep the place tidy.'

Captain Bones perked up at the mention of food and wandered over for a sniff. Valentine put the food behind the statue and stood the crate up on end to sit down on it. 'Perfect.'

Death puffed out his ribcage proudly.

'I should have thought of this earlier, really. Out of sight, out of mind. Anyway. I have to go. Work to do.' He flicked a spark to the end of his fingers and lit the candle.

'Can't I come with you?' It wasn't that he was spooked – he had grown accustomed to being surrounded by graves – but it was lonely in the graveyard. It made him remember how far away he was from the normal world, and all the people within it.

'Best not,' said Death. 'In case she's still lurking somewhere nearby. Tomorrow, maybe. You'll be fine here.'

'I don't want to stay on my own,' said Valentine.

Captain Bones gave a little yip of objection.

'There, see,' said Death. 'You won't be alone. Captain Bones will be here. And possibly –' he dropped his voice to a mumble – 'other company.'

'What?' said Valentine.

'Nothing. No one.' He took out his watch, flipped it open and closed it again so fast that Valentine was sure he hadn't checked it at all.

'What should I do if Linda comes?'

'She won't. This place is really well hidden. Believe me.' He chuckled. 'That's why I planted all those trees. No one has noticed it yet. Get some sleep. You shouldn't have any collections until daylight, and I'll be back by then. Hopefully. If not, set off without me.'

'But I—'

'Rush, rush, rush, Valentine, see you later, sweet dreams, bye-bye now.' He stepped through the closed door again.

'*Really well hidden*,' said Valentine to himself out loud. '*No

146

one has noticed it . . . But what was he hiding before me?'

'Us,' said a voice.

Valentine just about leaped out of his bones. He spun round. There was no one here. There wasn't anywhere to hide someone. Was there another tunnel below this floor, like in the mausoleum?

'Who said that?' whispered Valentine, crouching down next to Captain Bones. The dog gave his face an affectionate lick, then scampered over to the statue and started to sniff at Lady Clench's feet.

'Ugh! Get that ugly lump away from me.'

The statue was talking. Valentine backed away until he hit the door. 'Bones . . . Here, boy,' he called quietly.

The dog cocked his head to one side, thoughtfully, then resumed his sniffing.

'He's going to get slobber all over my jewelled slippers!' The lips of Lady Clench's effigy *actually moved*.

'Bones!' Valentine hissed, and this time the dog heeded his call.

'I don't mind house guests,' continued Lady Clench. 'But a little bit of notice would've been appreciated! Shocking manners.'

'Oh, I'm sorry, miss . . . umm . . . Your Highness?' said Valentine.

'I don't mean you, boy. I mean *him*. Ashamed of us, he is. Shuts us up out of the way like a dirty secret. And then, here's

147

a child for you to house, and not so much as a by-your-leave!'

'I'm not a child,' said Valentine. 'I'm an apprentice.'

'And I'm the Countess of High Roxbury,' she replied. 'For all the good it does me here.'

'Are you . . . ? Are you a ghost?'

'That's no question to ask a lady.'

'Were you the actual Lady Clench? Is this your grave?'

'Memorial, thank you very much. Commoners have graves.' She wrinkled her nose in disgust.

Valentine scratched his head, wondering how to phrase his next question. 'But . . . why are you still here? Why haven't you gone down to the Always?'

'You don't spend half your father's fortune on a memorial like this and then not spend some time enjoying it!'

'Are there more of you?'

'There's him.' She indicated upwards with her eyeballs. Valentine wondered if she could only move her face, since surely no one would lie in that position for a hundred years if they were able to move into a more comfortable one. 'Wickenham! WICKENHAM! Wake up, you useless oaf!'

'Leave me be, you ceaseless harridan,' the male statue responded. 'I had a glorious seven years of silence in here before you came along.'

'We've got company, Wickenham! It's the boy, you know, *the living one*.' She said the last three words in a whisper, as though they were too scandalous to be uttered in public.

'Boy, eh? Come closer, then, boy. Let's have a good look at you.'

Valentine approached, cautiously. 'So Death . . .' he began.

'Death knows that you're here.'

'Of course he does,' said Lady Clench. 'You wouldn't think it, though, by how rarely he stops by.'

'We're an inconvenience to him,' said Lord Clench. 'Spent the first thirty years trying to evict us!' He laughed. Like his wife, his facial features moved, but his body stayed stone-still. 'But nobody tells my good wife what to do – isn't that right, dear?'

'Correct, my love,' said Lady Clench. 'He was very keen that we go down and visit the museum.'

'Library, dear,' corrected Lord Clench.

'Don't interrupt, you bilious fool,' she answered sharply.

Lord Clench chuckled again. 'Can you imagine, child, centuries stuck in a crypt with this wretched old hag?'

'As I was saying,' Lady Clench cut in loudly, 'when he realized we wouldn't be moved, he hid us away, covered the front of our beautiful monument with ugly trees and pretended we didn't exist.'

'Is it too much to ask for the occasional visit?' agreed Lord Clench.

'You'll keep visiting us, won't you, dear?' said Lady Clench. 'You're not going to forget about us in another hundred years?'

'I'd be happy to visit you,' said Valentine. 'But . . . I won't

be alive in a hundred years.
I'll have to go back into the
Always before then.'

'You don't *have* to,' said Lord Clench.
'There's room for one more statue on that
bottom shelf.'

Valentine couldn't imagine anything
worse than being stuck inside a statue for ever with
these two people who either hated each other or were
deeply in love.

'What do you do to pass the time?' he asked.

'We sleep a fair amount,' said Lord Clench.

'A bit of singing, here and there,' said Lady Clench.

'A few rousing games of I spy!'

'Sometimes spiders come in, so we watch them making
their webs.'

'Barely time to fit it all in, really,' said Lord Clench.
'Speaking of –' he yawned loudly – 'you don't mind if I go
back to sleep, do you? Awfully tired.'

'Yes, that's right,' said Lady Clench. 'Early to bed, early
to . . . something, something. Goodnight, dear.' She
closed her eyes.

Valentine and Captain Bones shared a look of concern.
Knowing that the statues could see him made Valentine
reluctant to turn his back on them.

Lying on the floor was very uncomfortable. He tried sitting

up, resting his back against the wall, but that was as bad. He took off his cloak and folded it, trying to put padding between his bony bits and the floor – it helped a little, but now he was cold. With a quiet whimper, Captain Bones curled up beside him.

'I'm glad you're here,' Valentine whispered. As he waited for sleep to arrive, he checked his pocket watch. Philomena's hand was still there, edging backwards. He wished it would hurry up – he'd feel much better knowing she was far away from her death time. Another hand was halfway through the one-day section but edging ever closer to the hour section – there would be a collection due in the morning. 'And I hope Death is here when we wake up.'

Slipped Away

Valentine rose at the first light through the stained-glass windows. Lord and Lady Clench were still asleep – he could tell by the snoring sounds – but Death was nowhere to be seen, so he scooped up his dog and headed out.

They picked their way through the graveyard cautiously, heading back to the mausoleum. Maybe Death was there, depositing a soul or killing time before his next collection. But the mausoleum was dark and empty, the stone slab above the library stairs still firmly in place. Atropos, roosting in a coffin niche, opened her sharp eye at Valentine's arrival, and followed him back outside.

A fluttery, buzzy movement came from his jacket pocket. The watch, reminding him of his duties. It fell still as he opened the case and gazed at the hands. His collection was approaching quickly now, well into the hour section of the face.

Valentine decided to carry on with his day as if everything was fine. Which it probably was.

'Stay here, Bones,' he said. 'Back soon.'

He tapped impatiently on the other side of the watch. Was it his imagination or had the shimmering liquid inside begun stirring before his finger had even made contact with the glass? As he watched it swirl and form into the star shape, a pleasant, tingly sensation trickled down the back of his neck. It was a feeling he didn't have a name for. Peace? Purpose? Focus?

The star pulled to the right, and he turned and began moving in that direction. Atropos kept pace with him, flitting from gravestone to statue as they crossed the cemetery. 'You don't need to come with me,' said Valentine. He was sure the prickly, fierce creature had been warming up to him, until the Philomena incident had made her furious. 'It was a one-time thing. I won't do it again.'

The watch led him straight to the cemetery gate, and this time Valentine was doubly careful to lock it behind him.

They travelled through the market, further than he had been before, beyond the turning which led to Partridge Street and Philomena. He wondered how she was. He hoped that her soul had settled back into place now, and she could carry on with her life as normal.

Everyone Valentine passed was hard at work or walking with purpose. He was struck by the realization that every single one of these strangers was right in the middle of their own story, a hundred lives, all passing momentarily through the same space before spinning off into different directions.

And every single one of them, he thought, *is headed to the same place in the end.*

Though no one seemed to notice him, even when they nearly collided, he studied every face he saw. All their souls had been mixed together in the Always. Perhaps many times. And all of them would return to be mixed again eternally.

The watch trembled slightly in his hand. The star was glowing more brightly now – it was getting stronger as he got closer to his destination.

It finally led him down a back alley and into a house. In the downstairs room were two men, both staring anxiously towards a doorway. Neither noticed when Valentine entered, nor noticed the black crow who landed neatly on top of a tall cupboard.

Five minutes to go. Whoever it was, they were on the other side of the next door.

As Valentine stepped towards it, a woman came bustling through. A stout, grey-haired woman he instantly recognized – the woman from the graveyard. What was she doing here? She carried a cloth-wrapped bundle in her arms.

The bundle gave a feeble cry.

No. Please. Not a baby. Valentine couldn't do that. He felt sick. Atropos tilted her head to one side, meaningfully.

'A son,' said the woman quietly. She handed it to the nearest man, who looked terrified to hold something so small.

'How is she?'

The woman shook her head. 'It was a very difficult delivery. I don't know if . . .' She paused, her eyes briefly locking on Valentine's. 'She isn't going to make it. I'm sorry.'

'Will the infant . . .' the other man began. 'How will we feed him?'

'I think he will survive. A wet nurse – I know a woman. She'll see you right.' She glanced again at Valentine but didn't make his presence known to the men.

'Thank you, Mercy. I know you did your best for her.'

Mother Mercy.

Mercy. Mercy Dyer, the midwife – that was who Philomena worked for, wasn't it? What were the odds that Valentine was apprenticed to Death, and Philomena was apprenticed to Death's old friend?

Was Philomena here, too?

155

Valentine tried to clear his thoughts and tapped on the watch again. The star dissolved and a name began to form.

Thomasine Nash.

'Get it over with, then,' muttered the midwife under her breath.

Valentine nodded.

'I don't approve of this, for the record,' she said as he swept past her.

Thomasine Nash lay on a mattress on the floor of what might generously be called a kitchen. Her face was a shade too white for human skin, but she was past pain now, and appeared to be sleeping peacefully.

Valentine couldn't help wondering, was this how his own story had begun, too? His mother giving her last ounce of life to bring him into the world and then taking her own leave of it?

He knelt carefully beside the mattress. Atropos landed beside him. It seemed like she found this terribly sad, too, and that helped, somehow.

The woman opened her eyes very slightly and saw him, but said nothing. Her expression was one of resignation, as though she had known all along that this was when she would go.

'Thomasine Nash,' said Valentine.

She managed the slightest smile and gently nodded her head. Valentine consulted the watch. It was time.

156

Valentine Crow reaped the soul of Thomasine Nash. Then tucked it safely in his blacker-than-black cloak, and fled the house. Out in the unforgiving daylight, he took a moment to gather himself. Atropos landed on his shoulder.

'Thank you for coming with me,' Valentine said. 'That was a tough one.'

The crow leaned in and rested her feathery head against Valentine's cheek, just for a second. Then she straightened up, made a clicking sound and took off, swooping over the rooftops and leaving Valentine by himself.

Full of unwelcome emotions, he turned the next corner without looking and knocked against someone coming the other way.

'Sorry!' he called over his shoulder, pacing onwards.

'Valentine!'

He stopped. It was Philomena. He very much needed a friendly face but couldn't bear the thought of telling her why he was here.

'Valentine!' Philomena's voice was frantic. She ran the few steps to catch up and flung her arms round him. 'Thank goodness – you can see me!'

Given Up the Ghost

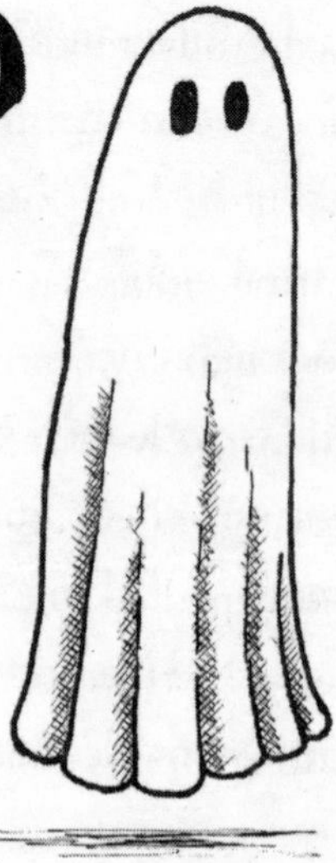

Valentine longed to hug Philomena back but didn't dare. Just outside her skin, her soul hovered, warm and viscous as honey. And after a moment her grip relaxed as she realized Valentine hadn't put his arms round her. She stepped back and he saw that she was crying.

'You *can* see me, can't you?' she asked.

'Yes?'

'Oh, Valentine, it's been awful.'

'What's happened?'

'This is going to sound mad, but . . . I think I've gone invisible.' She sniffed loudly and wiped her face on her sleeve.

'You what?'

'You don't believe me.' A sob came up from her chest

158

and she dropped her head forward and cried. Valentine, very carefully, touched her shoulder as lightly as possible to comfort her.

'I believe you, but I don't know what you mean,' said Valentine. 'I can see you, though.'

'Do I look . . . normal?'

Valentine nodded. 'The same as always. Except for the crying.'

She wiped her eyes again. 'And you can hear my voice properly? Nothing is different?'

'Nothing,' said Valentine. 'What's going on?'

'Remember when that horse and cart nearly flattened us?'

'Uh huh.' How could he forget the moment she was supposed to die?

'After that, I went home, and Maggy and Jo – the other girls who live at Mother Mercy's house – they couldn't remember my name.' She bit her nail anxiously. 'I thought they were having fun with me. But then they kept it up all afternoon. I thought it must have been because I dropped the clean washing and it needed doing all over again.'

Valentine was confused. It wasn't like Philomena to be so upset over a little teasing.

'I said I'd fix it myself. But they looked at me like they'd forgotten I was even there and started washing it on their own. Then Mercy's nephew came home, and he was the same. I asked how his day was and he squinted at me as if . . .

as if I was someone he used to know a long time ago, and he was trying to place me.'

'That's . . . odd,' said Valentine.

'Then this morning –' she sniffed loudly – 'none of them even looked at me. I clapped my hands right in front of their faces and they didn't even blink. I shouted their names. Nothing. And then I came out into the street, and nobody there seemed to see me either.'

There was a feeling in Valentine's chest like a rock dropped into deep water. 'Are you sure?'

'Watch.'

A man was approaching from the direction of the market, carrying a folded newspaper that he kept glancing at and frowning.

'Excuse me!' shouted Philomena. 'Sir? You there!'

The man didn't react. As he passed them, Philomena tugged at his sleeve. No response.

This was alarming. Valentine had become used to people not noticing him when he went on collections in his reaper cloak, but this wasn't the same thing. He was always able to make himself seen and heard if necessary, and they'd certainly hear him if he shouted.

'He's distracted by his reading,' said Valentine.

The man paused and looked back over his shoulder. 'Are you talking to me, boy?'

Valentine shook his head, and the man shrugged and

went back to his paper.

'See?' said Philomena. 'Look.'

She followed quickly until she caught up with him and knocked his hat off. He made a disgruntled noise and glanced over his shoulder again, then stooped to pick it up. He walked away with a puzzled expression, rubbing the back of his head. Philomena returned to Valentine's side.

'I've been trying to get strangers to notice me all day. None of it has worked. I'm really scared!'

Valentine could fix this for her now. Her soul was loose; he could slip it away in an instant and take her to the warm, comforting glow of the library, like he was supposed to have done. She wouldn't be scared there. She wouldn't feel ignored or invisible. Hesitantly, he touched the edge of her honey-coloured soul. If Death was here, he'd tell Valentine to take it.

But if he took her to the library, he'd have to leave her there, and she'd go into the Always and he'd never see her again. At least not in this lifetime, or in this form. And she was the closest thing he had to a friend.

The other soul, the one he had already collected, squirmed impatiently, as if to remind him of his duty.

'What's happening to me, Valentine?'

'I'm not sure,' he said, choosing his words carefully. He'd hoped that she would never find out about her should-have-been death time or the choice he'd made. But she deserved an explanation. 'But . . . I think . . .'

'Wait,' said Philomena. 'Mother Mercy!'

The midwife was trudging down the street in their direction, eyes on the ground, her short-legged gait stiff but determined.

'Mistress Dyer!' Philomena jumped up and down, waving both arms above her head. 'Mother Mercy!'

Mother Mercy paused and tilted her head to one side, as if listening intently.

'Mother Mercy!' Philomena called again and took off running towards the old woman. He followed her.

Mother Mercy looked up at Philomena, but her gaze slid right off her and instead her dark, birdlike eyes affixed on Valentine. She frowned.

'What are you still doing here? Don't you spend enough time on these streets already? You've got what you came for. Be off with you.'

'Mother Mercy, it's me, Philomena. Can you hear me?' Philomena pleaded. She hadn't yet noticed that Mercy recognized him.

Mercy squinted in concentration.

'Do you hear Philomena, Mother Mercy?' said Valentine. 'Can you see her?'

'Philomena?' said Mercy. 'Why do I know that name?'

'Your apprentice. From the Foundling Hospital!'

'No. I've got a Margaret. She's my apprentice for three years now.'

Philomena grunted with frustration and clasped Mercy's hand in hers. 'I'm here! I live in your house; how do you not know me?'

Mercy looked down at her hand and blinked with surprise. Her gaze travelled up Philomena's arm to her face, and when their eyes met, she smiled. 'Lovely to meet you, dear. From the Foundling Hospital, you say? Fine institution. Saved many an infant from falling into the wrong hands.' She shot Valentine a withering scowl, leaving him in no doubt whose hands she was talking about.

'Don't you remember? You picked me up from the hospital yourself.'

'Oh.' Mercy's forehead creased. 'An apprentice . . . How very odd, now that you say it . . . I recall . . . We came in a carriage, didn't we?'

'Yes! It let us out on the corner there.' Philomena let go of Mercy's hand to point to the place. 'And you complained that the driver had stopped right over a puddle.'

Mercy didn't respond and resumed her steady walk.

'Mother Mercy?' called out Philomena brokenly. 'Something is happening to me.'

'Why are you ignoring her?' said Valentine. It was easier to be angry with the old woman than to think about his own role in this disaster.

'Ignoring who?' said Mother Mercy. 'Stop bothering me with your nonsense, boy. Aren't there enough poor souls in London to keep you busy without having to torment me?'

Mercy Dyer stomped away without another word. Philomena stared helplessly at her retreating shape. Valentine stared helplessly at Philomena.

Now what?

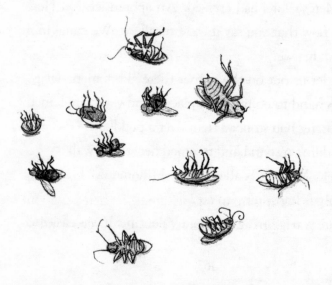

Taken to the BONEYARD

The soul in his cloak was getting restless. 'I have to go back home,' said Valentine.

'Take me with you,' Philomena replied immediately.

'It isn't . . . It's not very comfortable,' said Valentine. Even as he hesitated, he knew he couldn't leave her behind in this state.

'It can't be any worse than this,' she said. She tucked her hands into her armpits and Valentine didn't know if she was shivering from cold or panic. 'What else will I do? Haunt Mercy's house like a ghost?'

She touched his arm. 'Please, Valentine.'

He nodded. 'Yes. Of course.'

Valentine led her back to the cemetery gate in silence, both of them reeling from the weirdness of their situation. Philomena turned to check her reflection in every window and puddle, making sure she still had one.

He unlocked the graveyard gate and opened it.

'Why do you have a key to the churchyard?' asked Philomena.

Valentine shrugged. She'd find out soon enough.

Three steps beyond the gate, she stopped. Philomena gazed behind her through the gate and then forward again. 'Where's the church gone? How . . . ?'

Valentine closed the gate, being extra careful to make sure it was securely fastened.

'I don't understand. This isn't the same graveyard we could see from the road, but that's impossible.'

Valentine shrugged again. 'Apparently not.'

'So where are we?'

'Not sure. We're in London, but also . . . outside it.'

She pinched his arm.

'Ow! What was that for?'

'To test if I'm dreaming. Oh, sorry, that's the wrong way round. Here, you can pinch me back if you want.'

'I don't want to,' said Valentine. 'You're not dreaming. Listen, Philomena, when I met you for the first time at the market, I was telling the truth – I work for Death. I work for the Grim Reaper. And I can prove it. Put your hands out.'

She eyed him suspiciously but did as he asked.

'Keep really, *really* still,' said Valentine. Then he carefully took the soul out from his cloak and gently lowered it into her arms.

'What *is* it?' Philomena's eyes widened.

'A reaped soul,' said Valentine.

'It's warm,' said Philomena.

'Yes,' said Valentine. 'Most of them are warm.'

Philomena tentatively handed the now squirming soul back to him as though it might bite. 'Valentine, I have a lot of questions.'

'Join the club,' he muttered.

'Pardon?'

'Come this way.' He started walking towards the memorial. She'd be safe there with the Clenches while he took the restless soul down to the library. 'Ummm . . . I'm not really allowed to have you here. No one is supposed to come into the cemetery. No one alive, I mean. So, you need to keep hidden until we work out what's happening with your whole . . . invisible thing.'

'Hidden where?' Philomena lagged behind, taking in her surroundings nervously.

'There's a little, um . . . sort of house, behind those trees.'

'A house in the middle of a graveyard?'

'House-ish.'

He led her between the yew trees to the entrance of the Clench memorial, where Captain Bones sat eagerly monitoring the movements of a squirrel in the branches above. He yipped happily at Valentine and gave Philomena a welcoming sniff.

167

'This is Captain Bones,' said Valentine. 'Captain, this is Philomena. She's an old friend. From the Foundling Hospital.'

'Cute,' said Philomena. 'Mercy had a spiteful ginger cat. Dogs are much better.'

Captain Bones wagged his tail in agreement.

'Could you wait out here . . . for a second?' Valentine let himself into the memorial and closed the door as softly as he could.

'Scoundrel!' shouted Lord Clench.

'It's me!' Valentine protested.

'Call that a horse? Pah!'

'What—?'

'Ignore him, dear,' said Lady Clench in a bored tone. 'He talks in his sleep. You get used to it after a few hundred years of marriage.'

'Lady Clench, I've brought a visitor for you.'

'Ooooh, I knew you were the right sort, the moment I met you. Where is he, then?'

'She,' said Valentine. 'Her name is Philomena, and she needs somewhere to stay for a few days.'

'A little female company never goes amiss. I have all this womanly wisdom to pass on and no daughters to share it with. You see, back in my day—'

'Wisdom, yes, great.' Valentine couldn't afford to let Lady Clench go off on another lengthy speech. 'Only, the thing is, Death can't know that she's here.'

'Master Valentine, what are you up to? A little young to be courting ladies, aren't you?'

'We're not courting!' said Valentine, a bit too loudly. Hot blood rushed to his cheeks. 'Philomena's my friend. She had to leave home because . . . for complicated reasons. Will you keep an eye on her? She doesn't really understand all this stuff yet.'

'I don't approve of keeping secrets from your master, Valentine,' said Lady Clench disapprovingly.

'Oh . . .'

'On the other hand, I'm extremely bored, so, go and fetch her.'

'Thank you!'

Valentine opened the door and called to Philomena. On the threshold he was hit by a moment of doubt: one was a ghost, and the other was . . . a not-ghost . . . Would they even be able to hear each other?

'Seriously, Valentine? In a tomb? That's disgusting.'

'Memorial,' corrected Lady Clench.

'Who said that?!'

'That's—'

'Lady Clench, to you. And I'll have you know this is the most expensive memorial in the county. *Disgusting?* How dare you!'

'I . . . um . . .' Philomena froze at the doorway and looked to Valentine for help.

'This is the memorial of Lord and Lady Clench. They liked it so much they've decided to stick around for a few hundred years to enjoy it. Lovely, isn't it?'

He gave Philomena an intense stare and raised his eyebrows.

'Beautiful,' she said slowly, holding Valentine's gaze. 'When I said *disgusting*, I only meant . . . uh . . . disgusting that there's nowhere for us to wipe our feet before we come into such a fine place.'

'An excellent point, come to think of it,' said Lady Clench.

'Can I talk to you for a minute?' said Philomena.

Valentine nodded and they stepped back into the graveyard.

'Ghosts, Valentine?' Philomena whispered loudly. 'Actual ghosts?'

'Suppose so,' he said. 'But they're friendly, I promise. They haven't had many visitors recently.'

'Why didn't they warn us?'

'Who?'

'The Foundling Hospital! All those lessons about preparing us for the real world with hard work and quiet habits and humble expectations. Why didn't they tell us, "Shine your shoes, wash your face, oh and by the way there are *ghosts* out there and sometimes people turn invisible for *no reason!*"'

'Do you think they knew already?' said Valentine. The thought hadn't occurred to him. The bursar hadn't been happy about Death turning up to collect his apprentice . . . but no one had acted shocked to see him. All the dying people took it in their stride. And those who did notice Death – Mercy, for example – never seemed to panic the way he might

170

expect. Did all the adults know about this stuff all along?

'We used to get in trouble for pretending there were fairies in the long grass.' She waved wildly at the overgrown clumps of weeds between gravestones, as if the fairies might appear to prove her point. 'Matron said we had to keep our feet on the ground because the world was a hard place and there was no time for silly fantasies.'

'It *is* a hard place,' said Valentine, more to himself than to Philomena. 'It's not what I expected at all.'

'Me neither. Ghosts! This is the third impossible thing that's happened today,' said Philomena. 'And I haven't even had breakfast.'

'I can do breakfast!' Here at last was a problem Valentine could solve. 'I've got some food tucked away inside.'

'Inside the tomb?' Philomena looked sceptical.

'It's just a stone room, really,' he said. 'Don't think of it as a tomb.'

He opened the door and Captain Bones pushed between his legs to run inside. He must've heard the word 'food'. Perhaps there was a clever dog hidden behind the straggly fur and slobber.

Retrieving the bundle from its spot behind the

statues, Valentine spread it out atop the wooden box. Not that much, split three ways, but it would have to do. He threw some scraps to Bones and divided the remaining crackers and jam between him and Philomena, giving her the bigger share.

'Gracious, boy, is that it?' Evidently Lord Clench had awoken now, too. 'This fine lass deserves a better breakfast than that.'

'I'm doing my best,' said Valentine.

'Thank you,' said Philomena.

'Ah, do you remember, Wickenham, when we were first betrothed?' Lady Clench chimed in. 'You went hunting and presented me with the largest roasted boar I'd ever laid eyes on. And venison pie!'

'Venison pie!' Lord Clench exclaimed. 'See, son? That's how you woo a maiden!'

'I'm not trying to woo anyone!' Valentine hissed. He hoped Philomena hadn't noticed his cheeks going red, but she was focused intently on her own fingernails.

Lord Clench chuckled, fondly. 'We're trying to help you, lad. You may not believe it, but us fusty old relics were young once, too. I know what's on a young gentleman's mind . . .'

'Right! Got to go!' Valentine leaped hurriedly to his feet. 'Please stay here, Philomena; I won't be long.' He patted Captain Bones. 'Look after her, won't you? And please –' he turned to the Clench statues – 'don't embarrass me.'

It was a relief to be out in the cool air of the graveyard. His thoughts were all shaken up. What *had* he done?

Valentine headed for the mausoleum and belatedly remembered to pause behind a high headstone for a moment or two, to be sure that Linda wasn't lurking around. When he was satisfied that the path was clear, he let himself inside.

'Oh, there you are!' said Death. As far as Valentine could tell, he had just been stood in the dark, waiting. This was disconcerting. 'What took so long?'

'Ummm . . .' Valentine wondered if this was a trick. Perhaps Death had found out what he'd done and was wondering if Valentine would confess. That was a common trap at the Foundling Hospital, meant to teach them honesty. Whatever trouble you got in, it'd be double if you didn't own up at the first opportunity. Valentine didn't know what it'd be like to be in trouble with Death, though he feared he was close to finding out.

'Your collection was this morning – wasn't it? I thought you'd be waiting for me when I got back.'

The door swung closed behind him, casting the chamber into darkness.

'Right,' said Valentine. 'I had to . . . feed the dog.'

'Of course. Silly me. Dogs are always hungry, like humans. That must be why you get along so well. I came looking for you at the memorial. Must have just missed you.'

Phew. That was close.

'You managed all right, though? Got the soul, no problems?'

173

'Got the soul.' Valentine held it up, trying not to think about the collection itself. The soul gave off only the faintest light, barely enough to reveal his own fingers where they gripped it.

'Jolly good.' There was a rough scraping sound – Death must be lifting the slab to the staircase. 'Let's get them dropped off, then.'

Valentine shuffled forward, edging round the huge stone table. It'd give him a nasty bruise on the ribs if he bumped into it.

'Death, can we maybe light a—' But before he could get the words out, his toe had caught on the slab and he stumbled.

Automatically, he flung his arms out and the soul slipped from his grasp, flying towards the hole in the floor. Valentine lunged forward, catching the soul just before it plummeted out of reach and scooping it to his chest. But he was beyond the point of recovering his balance. His left foot came down on the edge of the opening, half on solid stone and half on empty air, and in he went.

Valentine thudded like a wheat sack on to the steps below, but his momentum was too great and he couldn't stop. Scrabbling his feet, he tried to brace himself, but he skidded and bumped down sideways until, some twelve or fourteen steps from the top, he slid . . . right off the edge.

In every catastrophe there is a moment of terrible clarity, when the world goes quiet and all that remains is the horrible anticipation of what is to come. A realization that disaster is imminent and inevitable. Valentine couldn't save himself from the unfathomable darkness.

but the plunge, the freefall, the monstrous descent had not yet begun.

It's often said that in the moment before death, your life flashes before your eyes. Valentine didn't have much life to flash. Instead, he thought about Philomena. Suspended above the abyss, he had time for exactly two thoughts. The first was that Philomena was alone in the memorial, and if Valentine didn't return, she'd never know what happened, or why she was invisible, and since nobody knew she was there, nobody could help her.

The second was,

'This is going to hurt.'

In the Eternity Box

Valentine closed his eyes as gravity began its work. All his insides sloshed together as he dropped over the edge. As he opened his mouth to scream, he was jolted sharply upwards by a rough tug on his shoulder. Death had caught him just in time.

He hoisted Valentine up on to the steps and lowered him gently back to his feet. The world spun the wrong way for a few seconds as Valentine's pounding heart and frantic lungs gradually realized that they were safe, and his trembling legs tried to remember how to hold his weight.

'Good catch,' said Death. Valentine wasn't sure if Death was talking about himself or Valentine, who was still miraculously clutching the soul he had dropped.

'You saved my life.' Valentine's voice came out squeakier than usual.

'Huh!' said Death. 'So I did. First time for everything, eh? Are you hurt?'

'No,' said Valentine, though he'd be covered in bruises by tomorrow.

'Sorry. I should have lit a candle. I forgot that you humans can't get around in the dark. Those weird, wet, squishy eyeballs of yours. Not very effective, are they?' He clicked his finger bones to produce a small light and began heading down the stairs.

'Have you really never saved anyone's life before?' asked Valentine.

'Of course not,' said Death. 'Not sure if you've noticed, kiddo, but that's the opposite of my job.'

'Right, but you've been around since for ever, haven't you?'

Death shrugged. 'Give or take an aeon, yes.'

'And you've never spared anyone?'

'We talked about this. It's not me that's making them die. It's the illness or—'

'Yes, yes, I remember,' said Valentine. The stairs seemed longer and steeper than before, and the blackness much blacker. 'But haven't you ever been tempted to do *something*? Stop them from getting sick, even?'

'I know that sounds like a good idea,' said Death. 'But it's not as simple as that.'

'But you saved *me*!'

'It's not your time yet.'

'So what would happen if I died before my time?'

'You wouldn't die before your time. I wouldn't take you.'

'But what if you did?'

'But I wouldn't.'

Frustrating. 'What if it *was* my time, but I didn't die?'

'It wouldn't happen, Valentine. Don't worry about it.'

They walked a few more steps in silence.

'In all of history, though,' Valentine tried again. 'Someone must have been forgotten or left behind at some point . . .'

Death reached the bottom of the stairs and turned. His face was level with Valentine, who was a few steps behind. 'Has something happened, Val? Did you forget a collection? Let's check your watch.'

'Nope!' Valentine swallowed hard. He couldn't show Death his watch until Philomena's hand had completed the return journey. A watch hand moving backwards would alert Death to what he had done. 'Everything is fine. I only want to understand so I can do the job better.'

Death didn't answer immediately, so Valentine filled the silence.

'At the hospital they said it was our duty to learn everything about our trade and do our masters proud.'

'And you're doing well.' He placed his hand on Valentine's shoulder. 'I've been unfair on you. I've pushed you too much, too quickly. You didn't know any of this existed a few months ago. I shouldn't have had you going off on collections alone yet. It's only because of you know who . . .'

Valentine hugged the soul to his chest for comfort. He was caught in a strange mixture of guilt and affection. He hated lying to Death, but he was also afraid – afraid of Philomena dying, and of being in huge trouble, and for the first time ever, of disappointing someone he wanted to please.

'It was wrong to keep it a secret that I'm not allowed an apprentice. I've put you in a precarious position and at the very least I should have let you know the facts. That's on me. And I'm sorry.'

'Oh,' said Valentine. No adult had ever apologized to him before. In his experience, when children did something wrong, they were punished, and when adults did something wrong, the children were still punished. 'Well, thank you.'

'And while we're being honest . . .' Death trailed off and looked away, straightening his cloak.

This was it. Death clearly knew Valentine was keeping something from him and he was waiting for him to own up. The boy took a deep breath and screwed up his courage . . .

'There's something else,' Death began, before Valentine had found the right words. 'It's not only that I'm not allowed to have an apprentice. It's . . . humans aren't supposed to be apprentices at all.'

'What? Why not?'

181

'They don't think humans can do it. They don't think you can understand the importance of what we're doing here. Because your brains are teeny tiny.'

'They are not!' Valentine folded his arms. 'I bet yours is no bigger.'

'I haven't got one. It's not an insult – those weird, damp little brains are what makes humans special.'

'Not little.'

'Humans are incredible at learning. But no one wants to hear about it. So old-fashioned.'

'Why did you make me your apprentice at all, then?'

'Because we're going to prove them wrong, Valentine! You and me! We're going to show them that humans can do the job. And so what if your puny little mortal bodies only last a handful of decades! Being alive is supposed to be about learning, and aren't you learning a lot?'

Valentine nodded.

'We could change everything. Instead of having a few of us doing the job for ever, we could have every human do it for one lifetime.'

'For a lifetime . . . ?' said Valentine. Seven years sounded bad enough.

'A tiny diversion on your cosmic journey. To learn the secrets of the universe. To keep the world turning. Wouldn't that be worth it?'

'So I would spend my whole life in a graveyard, only

meeting people when they die, is that your grand plan?'

'You're thinking too human. You need to think of it on a cosmic scale.'

'I can't,' said Valentine, 'because I *am* human. I can't imagine eternity. I can barely imagine one whole lifetime.'

'That's right,' said Death. 'Because of your damp little brain.'

'Hey!'

'Now you know everything I should have told you from the beginning. We can't be a proper team with secrets. Can you forgive me?'

'Yes,' said Valentine. He didn't trust himself to say any more than that.

Death extended his bony hand. 'No more secrets. Agreed?'

Valentine switched the dimly lit soul to his other arm and shook Death's skeletal fingertips, glancing away with shame. 'Agreed.'

Apart from the secret I'm already keeping . . .

'Come along, then, Valen-tiny-brain.'

A Note About Secrets and Lies

A lie is saying something you know is untrue to mislead or trick someone. A secret is saying nothing so that they believe something untrue all by themselves. So, when you think about it, secrets are just quiet lies. Most people will tell you that THEY are ALWAYS honest. Most people are liars.

Ceased to Be

The library was always peaceful.

As bleak and alarming as Valentine's situation was, it seemed much better in the soft glow of the library. He gently placed down the soul and watched as it formed into the shape of the woman again. His breath caught in his throat. Seeing her in human-ish form again brought back the terrible sadness of her collection.

'Thomasine Nash.' Her name came effortlessly to his tongue. 'I'm sorry for the bumpy ride.'

She smiled and stroked his cheek gently. 'That's all right; I knew it was my time. This place is so familiar.'

'I can help you.' A librarian was already at her shoulder, holding a small blue-and-orange book with Thomasine's name on the cover. They ushered her away and she didn't look back.

Not far away, Death was going through the same ritual with the souls he had collected. He had set two down and sent them off into the stacks, but still held on to the third.

'Oh dear,' he said.

'What's the matter?' said Valentine.

'This one, it's, um – this one isn't right. I need to take it somewhere. Out of the way. Excuse me?' he called to the nearest librarian. 'We need to use the . . . other place. You know.'

The librarian did know. 'Of course. This way.'

'Valentine,' said Death. 'You asked about the souls which are too wicked to go back into the Always. Do you still want to know?'

He hesitated before answering. Did he really want to know? The librarian was walking at a brisk pace and Death began to follow, holding the soul with both hands and at arm's length, as though it were a particularly vicious wild cat. Valentine hurried to catch up with them.

'It won't be very pleasant, Valentine. You can leave the library now and we won't have to talk about this for a long time yet.'

'I'm ready.'

The librarian had silently opened another door – not one of the eight which encircled the library floor, but a narrow one set into the bookshelves themselves so that, when closed, it was completely disguised.

They travelled down a completely featureless

corridor – nothing but grey on all sides. This too was illuminated by some unseen light source. Eventually it began to branch off, and doors appeared here and there, some of them half open. Valentine tried to peek inside, but the figures ahead of him were moving very fast and he had no chance to linger. There was an unnerving urgency in the way both Death and the librarian flew down the corridor.

Finally, the librarian glided to a halt and unlocked a door marked VACANT.

'I'll wait here,' they said.

'Thank you,' said Death. 'Valentine, last chance. You can choose to wait out here.'

'No, I want to know.'

'As you wish.'

The room was indeed vacant – no furniture whatsoever. It was hard to distinguish where the walls ended and the ceiling began.

Death put the soul down on the floor and took three strides away, sweeping Valentine back with him. The soul had begun to reform already, but there was something different.

The others had taken their human shape immediately, but this one was swelling slowly, unevenly, into something with the approximate shape of a human but with no clear features, no face or expression. Something with only the vaguest notion of humanness.

'As I thought,' said Death. 'This soul isn't going into the Always.'

'But where will it go, then?'

'The Never is coming. Valentine, quickly – can you sense it?'

Valentine listened as hard as he could, holding his breath

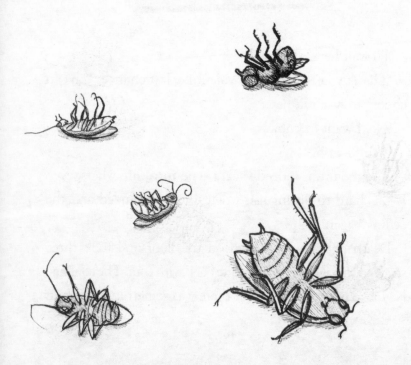

to make himself as silent as possible. 'I . . . I can't feel anything different.'

'Good,' said Death. 'Humans aren't meant to sense the Never. Only the soul it comes for, and the reapers. Take my hand.'

Valentine put his hand in Death's and *now* he could feel something. *Now he could sense it.*

'Death, it's here,' Valentine whispered.

'If you get too scared, let go of my hand and you won't see it any more. You're not in any danger. It doesn't know that you're here.'

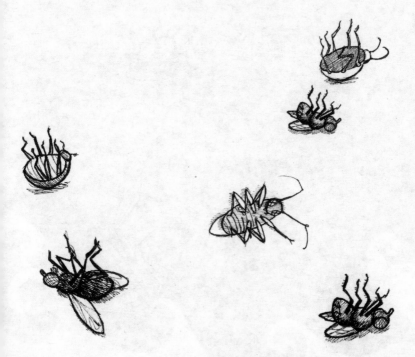

A Small Act of Mercy

What Valentine is about to witness is too frightening for those of a mortal disposition, so I will not describe it here.

I will not tell you how the ground beneath him begins to shift and tremble, nor mention the black smoke creeping round the doors and trickling down from the ceiling. I won't describe the breath-stealing sensation he feels, like plunging into water so cold it almost burns.

You don't need to know about the monstrous black form taking shape, or how it lumbers and lurches and staggers towards them, or the roar of the air rushing to fill the swelling emptiness.

You may imagine, if you wish, how tightly Death holds on to Valentine's hand, but do not think about the way that even Death shudders in horror at the Never. Do not try to picture the room growing darker as the Never consumes the light, or how time stretches until the gap between each heartbeat seems to last for hours.

For your own good, I will not write down the way the doomed soul cowers like a baby bird about to be eaten by a fox, or the terrible moment when the nothingness coils round it, twisting, smothering, crushing, first slowly and then all at once.

All I will say is this:

The Never came, and the soul was gone.

No Longer with Us

nd then it was over.

The room was back to normal. The soul was there no longer, and there was no trace of the entity that had devoured it.

Valentine let go of Death's hand and then snatched it up again, just to be sure. 'It's gone now, right?' he asked in a shaky voice.

'"Gone" isn't quite the right word. There has to *be* a thing for that thing to go away. And the Never is the opposite of a thing. And something that is not, and never was, cannot cease to be. It's more that the something that wasn't there while the Never was here – or wasn't here, technically – has come back. Understand?'

'Not even a little bit,' admitted Valentine.

'I did warn you,' said Death. 'You're not going to faint, are you? Or throw up? I hate it when people throw up. Why are your bodies so full of wet stuff?'

Valentine felt like his brain might throw up. 'What happened to the soul? Where is it now?'

'Doesn't exist. Removed completely from the universe.'

'Is it done?' The inscrutable librarian was in the doorway.

'Yes,' said Death, and together they left. The librarian locked the door behind them and silently disappeared down the corridor, as if they were physically incapable of making any noise.

Valentine and Death began to slowly follow after them. When they finally reached the door that led back into the library, Valentine summoned up the courage to ask the question that had been plaguing him.

'Death, how did you know that was going to happen?'

'It was cold.'

'Huh?'

'The soul. It was cold, and—'

'Most of them are warm,' Valentine finished. 'But if you knew, couldn't you just . . . not collect the soul? Then it wouldn't mix with the Always, but then it wouldn't have been . . . nothinged, either!'

'Evil people living for ever . . . does that sound like a good idea? The good people die, and the bad people keep living?'

'Oh,' said Valentine. 'When you put it that way, no, it doesn't.'

They were back in the main part of the library now, warm and bright and reassuring. It was as though the distress had been washed away from Valentine's brain, or at least muffled by layers of soft, papery comfort.

'It makes no difference anyway,' Death continued. 'The Never would have come for him eventually. People not dying at the right time, souls not being collected, that's a mistake, too. Sooner or later, the Never would come to fix it.'

A pit opened in Valentine's chest, bigger than the Never and the Always combined.

Philomena.

'But . . . what if it was a *good* person who didn't die when they were supposed to? Surely the Never wouldn't take them. They don't deserve it!'

'It's not about deserving or good and bad. The Never only knows about mistakes.'

'That's not fair!'

'The Never doesn't know about fair. Only—'

'Mistakes, I get it.' Valentine's mouth was dry. 'Is that why you said we should never be late?'

'That's the main reason. It's also very rude.'

'How – how late do we have to be before – before that happens?' How long had it been since Philomena should

194

have died? How long did she have left?

'Oh, a while, don't panic yourself. They won't be devoured if you take a wrong turn and get there five minutes late.'

'How long is a while?'

'I don't know, Valentine; I've never tested it. Because like you said – that wouldn't be fair, would it?'

'You must have an idea! Is it a day? A month? A year?' He must have been getting louder, because several librarians were staring furiously at them.

'Whoa there, Valentine!'

'You promised you'd tell me everything.' He felt a small pang of guilt at manipulating Death, while keeping a huge secret of his own. But it was nothing compared to the thought of Philomena falling victim to the Never.

'All right. Keep your britches on. At a guess, a week or two?'

A week. Hands on the pocket watch took one week to circle the dial and reach their final death time. It made sense that it would take seven days for Philomena's hand to travel all the way back. But that meant it wasn't counting her away from her death – it was counting her towards her extinction.

'The universe can cope with a little imbalance,' Death continued. 'It's like ripples on water. There's enough chaos and uncertainty at any given time that it evens out, a little bit. But if it goes on too long, the ripples become waves and threaten to sink the ship.'

'I'm confused – is the universe the water or the ship?'

'Both. Neither. I don't know. Anyway. You needn't worry about it. I wouldn't let that happen. If you ever miss a collection, tell me and I'll help you make it right.'

'How?'

'By taking the soul, of course.'

The Infinite Vest

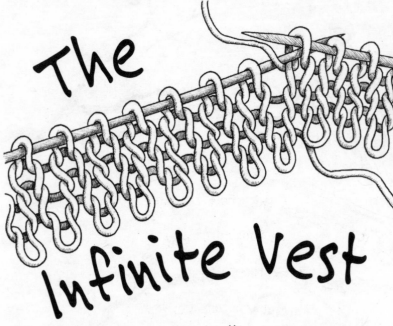

The universe is exactly like a knitted jumper. Viewed up close, it appears to be a huge number of separate and individual stitches. But cut the thread of even one of those stitches, and you will discover that the whole thing is one continuous string, delicately woven together in an intricate pattern.

A mistake – a dropped stitch, a corrupted soul, a disturbance in time – may seem **small** and **unimportant**, but it can dissolve the whole thing into chaos and tangled thread. The Never fixes mistakes. Without careful maintenance, the universe is prone to unravel like a woolly jumper snagged on a rusty nail.

Also, it is itchy and ill-fitting, and the colour does **not suit you.**

Lost at Sea

So he hadn't saved Philomena, after all. And either he confessed everything to Death and she died, or he kept it to himself and she was swallowed whole by the Never.

He would have to undo his mistake. Valentine owed her that. He would be honest about what had happened and why and she would understand. Maybe. Or maybe she would hate him for ever, and they'd meet in the next life as mortal enemies. If he told her today, maybe he'd spare her from the Never. Maybe he'd even be able to sneak her into the library without Death noticing. Maybe.

He shook off his thoughts and realized he was alone in the middle of the library, Death having already gone through the door to the staircase. Valentine headed out too, yearning to get back to Philomena and also dreading the moment. Valentine made his way up the stairs, trying very, very hard not to think about his near miss a few hours earlier. The swish of Death's cape had already disappeared into the gloom above.

A minute or two later, Valentine reached the top.

The slab had been replaced. He put his hands on it and pushed, but it barely budged. He climbed a little higher and turned his back, bracing his shoulders against the stone and pushing upwards with his whole body. It shifted a tiny bit, then stuck. He heaved and twisted and wrenched and shoved until his hands were sore from the rough stone, but no matter what he tried, he couldn't lift the slab an inch. Opening it completely was beyond hope.

He banged on the slab with his fists. 'Death? Are you there? Death?!'

But there was no response. Death could be anywhere by now.

With no chance of dislodging the slab, Valentine returned to the library.

'Excuse me,' Valentine called to the nearest librarian, who was rearranging books on a shelf directly below him. 'Could you come up and help me open the door to the mausoleum, please?'

'No, Valentine Crow. The librarians do not go any closer to the mortal world. It has been decided we must remain separate from it.'

'Does that mean that you can't? Or does it mean that you won't?'

The librarian simply blinked slowly and then turned away.

'Is there another way out, then? Back to London?'

'Out? Yes. To London?' said the librarian. 'No.'

Nobody was going to come along and fix things for him. If he couldn't get out through the usual doorway, maybe he could use one of the others and find his way back on the outside, somehow. He ran to the nearest door and yanked it open.

Valentine was in a tunnel. Every inch of the rough, yellow stone walls was covered in elaborate carvings of people and animals, and row upon row of mysterious symbols. He wasn't in London any more – perhaps not even in England. Almost certainly too far to get back to Philomena. Just in case, he continued on. The tunnel made several sharp turns before it reached two huge doors, three times his height. With great effort he pushed one open and was instantly hit with a wave of thick, dry heat. He was standing on a stone step, but before him lay nothing but sand, featureless and empty, and blazing, burning sun.

This was no use. He closed the door again and ran back down the corridor, then emerged, panting and sweaty, back into the library.

Valentine tried another. This door opened directly on to the side of a dizzyingly steep hill, rocky and treeless. The air here was cold – colder than London at this time of year – and the peaks of the neighbouring mountains were covered with snow. Huge birds with vast black wings and yellow-feathered bodies soared overheard, circling over a spot behind the crest of the hill. Valentine had no desire to find out what they were interested in. Wherever this was, it was nowhere near Philomena.

Carefully avoiding the Always, Valentine explored the library doors. Already he was fairly sure that none of them were going to be of any use – but with nothing else to try, he persisted. One opened on to the banks of a sunset river, and on the far shores great funeral pyres were burning. The next brought Valentine into something that more closely resembled the graveyard he was used to, although the letters on the stones were unfamiliar and a man with a broom gestured angrily at him and shouted something in a language he had never heard before. The next door took him to a chamber so utterly black that he had to stumble, arms out, until he located the door back to the library. The last door, then, his final hope.

He stepped through. He was on a rock, slippery and slimy, above a tumultuous grey ocean. He craned up at the tall, forbidding building behind him – it was a lighthouse, and that meant wherever he was, it was somewhere remote and inaccessible. Before he could retreat, a great wave crashed over the side of the rock, icy water instantly drenching him to the bone and knocking him off his feet so that he fell – luckily – back into the library.

He scrambled to close the door and wiped wet hair away from his face with his even wetter sleeve.

Think, Valentine. Think.

If he couldn't get out – and it seemed he was stuck here until Death returned – perhaps he could use this to his advantage. Maybe he could come up with a plan to bring Philomena back to life or to ward off the Never so he didn't have to take her soul after all.

There had to be something he could do. He was in a library that contained every human life that had gone before. The solution must be in one of these books – but which one? He gazed up at the rows and rows of bookcases stretching upwards to dizzying heights. It would take him hours to read one of those books – a hundred thousand years to read them all. And he only had a few days, at the very most, before Philomena met an unspeakable end.

A librarian passed by carrying two large volumes as if they were feather-light.

He couldn't ask a librarian, could he? They might be duty-bound to turn him in at once to Death and tell him what Valentine had done. Or else they might go ahead and summon the Never.

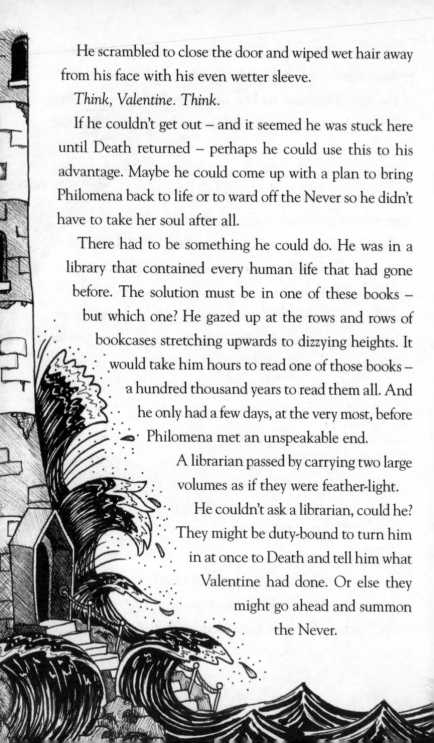

Maybe he didn't have to tell them, though. Maybe he could get them to help him find the right book . . .

'Excuse me,' he said to the next librarian he saw. Or perhaps it was the same librarian – Valentine couldn't remember what the other had looked like. 'Do these books contain everything that happened in someone's life?'

He leaned against a table, trying to act casual, as if the question didn't hold someone's entire existence in the balance.

'That's right,' said the librarian.

'Could somebody look up a specific day, for example, and see what happened?'

'If that's the answer their soul desires.'

'And if I looked up tomorrow in my book, could I see what's going to happen next?' If he could read ahead in his own book, maybe it would tell him how, or if, he was going to save Philomena.

The librarian blinked

and their eyebrows twitched the tiniest amount, the smallest flicker of curiosity or concern on their otherwise tranquil face.

'That is not the purpose of the library.'

'Of course not,' said Valentine. 'But could I, though?'

'The book entitled *Valentine Crow* is not yet complete. When the book is complete, there will be no more tomorrows for you.'

'Can I see it?'

'You will receive your answers when your time on Earth is done. This is the way of the library.'

The librarian smiled serenely, then nodded and continued off towards the bottom of a spiral staircase. Valentine darted over to the opposite side of the library and approached another librarian. Valentine watched silently as the librarian patiently cleaned and re-shelved a few more books, then turned and walked away. Valentine wandered between bookcases until he found another one nearer the entrance door. Or perhaps it was the first librarian again – he couldn't remember what they looked like.

'Is there a list of all the books in the library?'

'There is not.'

'How would I find a particular book?'

'Valentine Crow, we will always be here to assist.'

Valentine couldn't tell if the librarians were really as neutral and calm as they appeared or if they were actively trying to thwart him. 'I thought the library was all about answers.' He tried very hard to keep his tone casual and light, but desperation was beginning to slip out. 'Anything your soul wants to know. So why will nobody answer my questions?'

'That only extends to the dead, Valentine Crow. You are still alive.'

The librarian smiled their wretched smile and turned away.

Frustrated and exhausted, Valentine slumped down on to the floor. Somewhere in this room there had to be a book that could tell him how to fix this situation. His eyes drifted to the nearest shelf, and he saw a familiar name.

Thomasine Nash. The last soul he had taken. He sat up a little straighter. Two shelves up – Lucretia King, the woman from the duel.

The recently deceased were all shelved here. And if they were here . . .

The doorway to the library swung open. In the second and a half it took to open all the way, Valentine lurched through many different emotions: relief, that he could get back out to Philomena; panic, that Death might have found her already and be coming down here to deliver her soul; and fear, that it might not be Death at all, but Linda.

'Forgot you couldn't open the slab door with those puny human arms, Valen-tiny,' said Death, his echoing voice filling the whole space.

Tucked beneath his right arm, tongue hanging out, was Captain Bones.

'Your stinky little familiar here pointed it out to me. Scratching and barking and tugging on my cloak until I realized you were stuck down there.'

'Well done, boy.' Valentine took Bones and gave him an affectionate ear scratch.

'Onwards and upwards, then.' Death clapped Valentine on the back. 'Ew. You're all soggy.'

Valentine tried to think of a reasonable explanation, but Death didn't seem to care why.

'Come on, then, back up Earthside.'

'Coming.' Valentine hung back, moving as slowly as he dared, frantically scanning the shelves.

It was there. Right in the bottom corner, the book that hadn't been picked up in time. He grabbed it. It was thick but fortunately not too tall or wide. It fitted into his cloak pocket neatly, the weight of it pulling the fabric askew. He hoped it wouldn't get too damp before he had time to stash it somewhere safe.

Valentine's book wasn't complete yet, but Philomena's was.

'Shhh,' he whispered to Bones. 'Don't tell anyone.'

'Valentine!' Death's voice echoed through the open doorway. 'Keep up!'

Valentine jogged out. He expected someone to stop him, or shout that he was stealing a book, but the library remained as quiet and peaceful as always.

Death was already at the slab door, feet on the third step and the top half of his body disappearing through the gap. By the time Valentine reached the top, he was thoroughly exhausted. The mausoleum, as always, was stone cold and quickly sucked any warmth from Valentine's body through his wet clothes. He began to shiver.

'Outside,' said Death. 'Get the sun on you before you freeze.'

It wasn't the warmest day, but much better than the shady, rock-chilled indoors.

'Take your cloak off; you'll dry quicker.'

'It's fine; I'm not that wet,' said Valentine, shaking away the drop of water that had trickled from his hair down to the tip of his nose. Atropos hopped down from the mausoleum roof and shook her head disapprovingly.

'Here, I'll drape it over a headstone for you—' Death reached for Valentine's cloak and Valentine jumped back, his arms firmly folded.

'No!' The blocky shape of the book would give him away in an instant.

Death looked at him for a long moment. 'Please yourself, then. Don't catch a chill and die.'

'I'm not going to die, though, am I?' said Valentine. 'You told me that when I nearly fell off the stairs . . .' And the realization dawned on him as he spoke. 'I reckon I can do whatever I please for now, since it's not my time.'

'Humans are not meant to know these things.'

'Humans are not supposed to be apprentice reapers, either,' said Valentine. Whether it was the cold or the worry or his new-found determination to take matters into his own hands, he felt very annoyed by the whole Death-apprentice situation.

'Hm,' said Death. 'Fair point. But don't do anything stupid. Just because you're not going to die, doesn't mean you can't get really, really hurt.'

Post-mortal

The moment Death headed off to his next collection, Valentine ran over to the memorial. Atropos followed suspiciously, as though she knew he was up to something.

He hesitated outside the door and examined the book. Opening it to the end, he skimmed the writing. It was a description of the runaway cart accident – how it was supposed to have happened, anyway. It continued almost to the very edge of the very last page, but there was enough room to squeeze in a few words.

'It can't be that simple, surely?' he muttered. If the book was everything that happened, could he just change the book? He glanced up at Atropos, who was perched on the wing of a broken statue. 'Is that the answer? If I write in the

211

book that she lives till she's seventy . . .'

Atropos shook her head, unimpressed.

But it was worth a try. If it worked, he could go back to Philomena with good news instead of a horrible confession.

'What can I write with?' Nobody in the graveyard was in the habit of sending letters. 'Maybe I could mix up some mud. Or I've got some blackberry jam inside . . .'

Atropos cawed and shook her head again.

'But what about a pen?' He thought about dipping his finger in the jam and tracing the words with that, but the space was so small he was sure he'd end up with nothing but smudges. Something told him sticky smudges in a life book would not be a good idea. He needed something thin and hollow like a quill.

Or an actual quill.

'Atropos,' said Valentine. 'I need a feather.'

She clicked, puffed up her chest and turned away.

'Please? It's really important!' He took a step towards her and with a squawk she took off, up over the yew trees and out of sight.

Before he had time to think of a new solution, he heard

the click of the memorial door opening. Hastily he shoved the book back under his clothes. The sight of Philomena's worried face at the door brought his focus back to his task.

'You're soaked,' said Philomena, as Valentine entered. 'What happened to you?'

Valentine shrugged off his cloak and let it fall with a wet, sludgy thud on to the ground. 'I got hit by a big wave next to a lighthouse.'

'Lighthouse?' said Philomena.

'It's a long story. I've been to the library.'

'We've told her all about the library, son,' said Lord Clench.

'And the Always,' added Lady Clench. 'Filled her in on all the particulars.'

Philomena nodded. 'I don't completely understand yet, but I'm trying. Do you think we can use the library to find out why no one can see me?'

He cleared his throat, nervously. He had to be honest with her. They didn't have time for anything else. 'I already know the answer to that one.'

'You do?! Well done, Valentine!' She sounded so relieved and happy.

'I stole this book.' Sticking his hand in the bundle of wet fabric, he untangled the book and handed it to her silently.

For several seconds she stared at the cover, and Valentine stared at her, chewing on his bottom lip and bracing himself for the reaction that was sure to come.

'So, if it's . . .' She lightly touched the writing on the cover with trembling fingers. 'That means that . . . But it . . .' She looked up questioningly. Her brow was furrowed, and her brown eyes were wide and shiny. He watched the realization creeping up on her like a wave on the ocean, gathering speed and force and ready to drag her under.

'I'm sorry,' said Valentine.

'Am I going to . . . ?'

'You should have, already.'

'Don't keep us in suspense!' Lord Clench shouted.

'What is it?' said Lady Clench. 'We can't see from over here, you know.'

'It's my book,' answered Philomena. 'The book that isn't finished until *I'm* finished.'

'Oh, I see,' said Lady Clench.

'I don't!' said Lord Clench.

'Hush now, Wickenham!' Lady Clench hissed. 'You never know when to stop talking.'

Philomena turned the book over in her hands, as though she was afraid to open it. 'When—oh, the horse? You really *did* save my life, then.'

'I got there a few minutes early and saw you were healthy, and I thought, if I can stop whatever accident she's about to have, then . . . then I won't have to take her soul at all.'

'Oh, Valentine,' said Philomena. The tone of her words was like new socks, warm blankets, marmalade on toast. She went to hug him and his heart leaped, but he stopped her and stepped back. She needed the full truth. He hoped it wouldn't make her hate him for ever.

'But it turns out that was a bad thing. I shouldn't have done it.'

'So you'd rather I was dead?!'

'No! That's the last thing I want! But, missing your time of death is a really big problem. That's why people stopped seeing and hearing you. Why they don't remember you. You've become a mistake in the universe.'

She recoiled at this and screwed her face up with offence and hurt.

'I don't mean that *I* think you're a mistake!'

'Goodness, boy! This is no way to begin a courtship,' said Lord Clench.

'It's not a courtship!' Valentine protested. 'I'm sorry, I know

215

it sounds awful. But even though I meant to help you, I've messed things up.'

'You? You did this to me?'

He nodded.

'How do we make me properly alive again?'

'I don't think we can,' said Valentine.

'So I'm a ghost for ever?'

'It's not so bad, pet,' Lady Clench said. 'You can stay here and keep us company.'

Philomena kept her back towards the statues and mouthed *'no way'* to Valentine.

'It's worse than that.'

'Worse?!' Philomena groaned. 'Worse than being half-dead and invisible and living in a tomb for ever with the Clenches?'

'There's a thing that . . . corrects mistakes in the universe. It's called the Never, and it's a great black hole that hunts people down. It un-makes them. They don't go into the Always or get another life. They just *aren't* any more.'

Philomena said nothing. She hugged her book to her chest, arms wrapping round her shoulders as if she could hold herself together.

'And . . . and now that you're a mistake in the universe, it's going to come for you, too.'

'How do we stop it?'

'I think the only way to stop it is to . . .' He nodded and

shrugged, hoping she would get the point without him having to say the words.

'Is to what?'

'You know . . . do what I was supposed to do.'

'Wait,' said Philomena. 'You're saying that either I let you take my soul, or I wait for the big black whatever to come and kill me and *also* swallow my soul?'

'Um. Yes?'

Philomena clenched her teeth and exhaled sharply. 'You're right, Valentine. You messed up. You did something terrible. And you shouldn't have done it.'

Even though he understood why she was angry, her words stung like a slap to the face.

'I didn't mean to—'

'It doesn't matter whether you meant it or not. You did it. At least if I'd gone the way I was supposed to, it would've been over quick. I wouldn't have seen it coming. You should have done your job!'

'I didn't know! I didn't know any of this would happen!'

She shot him a final look of utter disgust before storming right past him and out of the door into the graveyard.

'Wait. Where are you going?'

'Away!' she called back, striding in a random direction away from the memorial.

'Come back!' He ran after her.

'Leave me alone.'

'You have to come back. You can't wander about! Death might find you!'

'If only Death had found me to begin with, instead of sending a stupid little boy to do his job!'

'Please, let me help you.'

'Look what happened last time you tried to help!'

'It was an accident!'

'No. Being trampled by a runaway horse would've been an accident. This was a mistake.'

'Mena, please!' He hopped over a toppled statue to get in front of her. She changed direction and kept walking. 'I don't want you to die. I care about you. You're my only friend.'

'I am *not* your friend.'

'But isn't it better that *I* take your soul? At least you get to come back and have another go at living. If the Never gets you, it's all over. For ever.'

'That's my choice, isn't it?' said Philomena. 'I don't need you making any more choices for me. I should get to decide for myself.'

'It's not a choice!' Valentine pleaded.

'Leave me alone!' She shoved past him and marched off between the headstones.

'Where are you going?' he shouted after her. 'You won't be able to get out!'

He sank down on to the plinth at the base of a huge marble cross. He expected her to turn back at any moment – what else could she do in a giant graveyard that isn't really anywhere?

But she didn't. Eventually she disappeared out of sight behind an ancient yew tree with wide, low branches that drooped as though it were tired after four hundred years of carrying their weight. After sitting for a few minutes longer, Valentine trudged back towards the memorial.

'That didn't go very well, did it, son?' said Lord Clench.

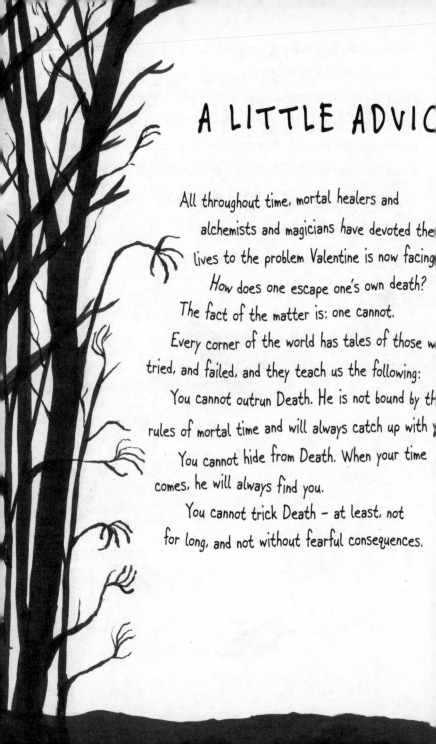

A LITTLE ADVIC

All throughout time, mortal healers and
alchemists and magicians have devoted the
lives to the problem Valentine is now facing
How does one escape one's own death?
The fact of the matter is: one cannot.
Every corner of the world has tales of those w
tried, and failed, and they teach us the following:
You cannot outrun Death. He is not bound by th
rules of mortal time and will always catch up with y
You cannot hide from Death. When your time
comes, he will always find you.
You cannot trick Death — at least, not
for long, and not without fearful consequences.

ABOUT DEATH

That said, many folk-tales suggest that Death has a playful side, and long ago it was said that he might grant more time if you beat him at a game of cards, or chess, or wits.

Should you wish to try this, I offer you one piece of advice. Whatever you do, never challenge Death to a pillow fight . . .

You can't handle the reaper cushions.

Fell Off His Perch

Valentine sat down on the cold floor. He was drying off a little, but the chill had already set in, right down to his bones. He would do anything for a warm cup of barley soup back at the Foundling Hospital.

Poor Philomena.

'All those people who've gone before us,' he muttered, 'surely one of them must've found a way to avoid Death.'

'Can't prevent Death, son,' said Lord Clench. 'That's the one thing that's a certainty in life.'

'That's right,' added his wife. 'And you can't bargain with him or cheat him either. When it's your time, it's your time.'

Valentine did his best to ignore them.

'Though there was that one cheat . . .' said Lord Clench.

'Oh yes, *that* one. The less said about her, the better,' said Lady Clench.

'What's that?' said Valentine, suddenly paying attention. 'Who? Who cheated Death?'

'I don't remember her real name,' said Lady Clench. 'But they called her Mother Misery.'

'Because she was a miserable old hag,' added Lord Clench.

'Yes. She cheated him, all right. Kept him prisoner in a cage in her kitchen.'

'No, no, that's not right. It was an old cloth sack. Or was it a magical cherry tree?'

'A plum tree?' Lady Clench suggested.

'I'm sure it was a cherry tree.'

'It doesn't matter what kind of tree,' said Valentine. 'What happened?'

'She stuck him there, and she wouldn't let him down until he agreed to never make her die. He was up there for what . . . a good four years?' said Lady Clench.

'More like forty!'

'Dreadful time.'

'No one could die. People were dragging themselves along getting older and older, no rest for those folks who needed it.' Lord Clench sighed as though the thought alone left him weary.

'In the end, he agreed. He changed things so her time would never come. And she released him and Death got back to work, and everyone was very relieved, for a little while. Before they all went back to hating him again, that is.'

'But how? How did she do it?' Valentine was up on his knees now, ready to jump into action.

'Beats me,' said Lord Clench.

'Some kind of nasty, horrible trick,' said Lady Clench.

'It can be done, then? A life can be extended?' Hope soared inside of him. If it had happened once, it could happen again.

'They say she's still out there,' added Lord Clench. 'Hundreds of years later. Wandering the earth because she can never pass on.'

'I don't think that's a fate you'd want for your friend,' said Lady Clench.

'But if a life can be extended for a long time, then surely it can be extended for say fifty years – that's not much, compared to for ever. Tell me everything. I need to know what to do.'

'That's all I know,' said Lord Clench with a yawn.

'Valentine?' a distant voice called. It was Death.

Valentine went outside to meet him.

'Everything in order?' said Death. 'I'm just popping back between collections. Oodles of souls today!'

'Can I ask you something?' said Valentine, pacing alongside Death as he headed towards the cemetery gates.

'Of course. We agreed. No secrets. Full honesty. Right?'

'Right . . .' said Valentine, a knot of guilt tightening round his ribcage. 'What did Mother Misery do to keep from dying?'

'Oh.' Death's arms dropped to his side, deflated. 'When I said no secrets, I meant, nothing that concerns the two of us. You don't need to worry about Mother Misery.'

'It's true, then? That she doesn't have to die?'

'I don't want to talk about it. It was a very embarrassing incident for me.'

'But you *promised* you wouldn't hide anything.' The guilt knot squeezed a little harder.

'Fine. I'll tell you. But don't go gossiping about it. It took me centuries to live it down.'

'I won't,' said Valentine. 'What happened?'

'I come to this cottage with a little old lady inside. She's teeny tiny, only about yay-high, barely there at all.' He indicated with his hand.

'Hey, that's my height!'

'Exactly,' said Death. 'And when I tell her it's time to go, she asks a favour. There's a tree in her garden that's been there all her life and has brought her so much happiness. She longs to taste the fruit one last time, before she passes over.'

'What kind of fruit was it?'

'Why does that matter?'

'The Clenches couldn't remember.'

'The Clenches.' Death put his hand over his eye sockets and shook his head. 'I might've known they'd tell you about this. They never could keep their mouths shut. It was an apple tree.'

225

'They said it was plums or cherries.'

'It was an apple tree. I should know. I was stuck staring at the cursed things for all that time.'

'She asked for an apple?'

'Yes. Not any apple, but the biggest, juiciest, most perfect one from the very top of the tree. Of course, she couldn't climb the tree herself. She was old and stiff; she even had a limp. I thought, what's the harm in granting an old woman's last wish?'

'Go on . . .' Valentine urged, struggling to bear the suspense.

'I climbed up the tree – which wasn't easy – I used to carry a scythe with me in those days and it really got in the way. And I picked the apple and passed it to her and then when I tried to get down—'

'You we're stuck!'

'How was I supposed to know she'd had the tree enchanted? There was a spell on it. Anything that climbed up there couldn't get back down until she gave her permission. She'd made a bargain with some sort of travelling wizard—'

'Wizards aren't real,' said Valentine.

'With some sort of travelling magic pedlar, who had put the spell on the tree for her. I don't remember why. She probably tricked him into it, too. She was that type of person. Very sneaky.'

'There's no such thing as magic spells, though.'

'Do you want to hear the story or not?'

'I do. Sorry.'

'Whatever you call it, somehow, this apple tree had the power to hold me there until she allowed me down. And considering why I had visited her in the first place, she wasn't all that keen on freeing me. I was stuck up there all night. Missed my next few collections, but it wasn't too serious, yet. I told her, you've had your fun, finish off whatever it is you've got to finish off, and say your goodbyes, it's time to go. But she wasn't having it. A few more days passed. A couple of squirrels were stuck up in the tree with me too, and they weren't pleased either.'

'How long were you up there?'

'Years. And everyone came to gawk at me! They would point and laugh at my bony fingers.' He shook out his wings indignantly. 'But they were furious at the old woman – she'd betrayed them. People were living long past their natural lifespans. Their souls knew, even if their minds didn't, that they were missing the Always. Their kindred spirits were calling to

227

them from the great beyond. Their bodies were worn out.'

'Oh no,' said Valentine, picturing poor old Gideon Pike on his deathbed, and how ready he was to move on to the next stage of his existence. A whole village, a whole city, a whole *world* of Gideon Pikes stuck that way for years and years.

'Honestly, I think even Mother Misery was feeling it by that point. She knew, deep down, that it couldn't go on, but she's the most stubborn human I've ever met. It was her way, or no way at all. So, when the people of the town began to turn on her and blame her for every problem that arose, she came to me with an offer.'

'Yes?' Valentine was leaning in, hardly managing to breathe as he waited for the answer that would surely save Philomena.

'She would let me down, and I could take all the other souls, if I promised she would never die.'

'And you did?'

'What choice did I have?'

'You could've just told her that and taken her soul anyway.'

'How dare you. That would be lying! I don't lie.'

'So, you *can* do it, then?'

'Lie? Only if I absolutely have to, like when someone gets an ugly haircut and you tell them it's flattering.'

'No,' said Valentine, 'you can make it so that people don't have to die?'

'No.'

'But—'

'Everybody has to die, Valentine! It's not optional. I should never have agreed to her terms. It was a mistake.'

'Mistake,' Valentine echoed. 'Does that mean she got taken by the Never?'

'No,' said Death. 'She's still around.'

'Why not, then?'

'I made an edit. Changed her time of death officially, in the records.'

Valentine straightened up sharply. 'How? How do you do that?'

'I don't, any more. It was a one-time thing. I regret it. And to tell you the truth, I think Mother Misery regrets it, too.' He flicked open his pocket watch. 'Valentine, I know you're having a hard time with becoming the bringer of death to all of humanity, and I get that. But I have a collection to do, and it's a big one. We'll talk about this another time.'

'I'll come with you,' he said. 'We need to talk about this now.'

'You can't come on this one,' said Death. 'The working conditions aren't safe for your fragile human flesh.'

'I'll stand at a distance, then. Please—'

Death shook his head, pulled his hood up and over his face, and collapsed into himself until Valentine was alone.

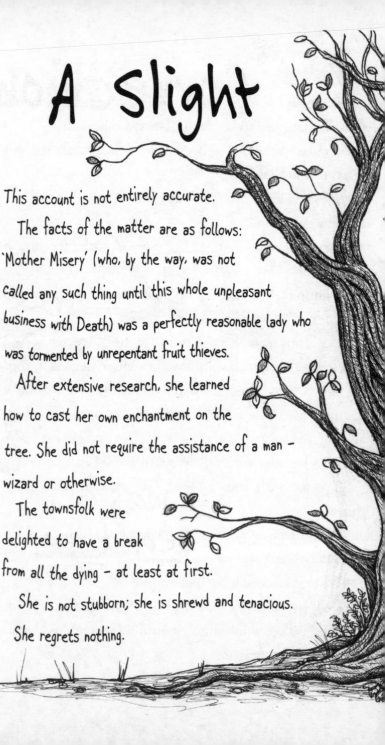

A Slight

This account is not entirely accurate.

The facts of the matter are as follows:
'Mother Misery' (who, by the way, was not
called any such thing until this whole unpleasant
business with Death) was a perfectly reasonable lady who
was tormented by unrepentant fruit thieves.

After extensive research, she learned
how to cast her own enchantment on the
tree. She did not require the assistance of a man –
wizard or otherwise.

The townsfolk were
delighted to have a break
from all the dying – at least at first.

She is not stubborn; she is shrewd and tenacious.

She regrets nothing.

Gently Decomposing

Death claimed that lives couldn't be extended, but admitted that it had been done once before. Not impossible, then. A small chance was better than no chance at all.

A small chance could save her.

Valentine marched over to the memorial, but as he ducked under a low-hanging yew branch, he was stopped by Philomena.

'Mena! You're back!'

'Yes, I'm back and you were right. Go ahead and do it quickly, please,' she said in one breath, barely a pause between the words. Philomena closed her eyes tightly and balled her hands into fists by her side.

'You want me to . . . ?'

'Yes, Valentine, take my soul. Get it over with.'

'Hang on a minute, we can keep trying – Death says it might take a week for the Never to find you and I've found out—'

'Death is wrong.' Philomena opened one eye, and then both. She didn't look at all well. 'Something's happening to me, Valentine. It's getting worse.'

'What is?'

'Everything. I think it's coming. I think I've seen it.'

Valentine shuddered. 'What did you see?'

'Not a lot, but I know that it's bad. I was way over in the corner of the graveyard –' she pointed off in a direction Valentine had not yet explored – 'and something was leaking in through the railings.'

'What was it like?'

'It looked like . . . like the tiniest drop of black ink spreading out in a bucket of water.'

'The Never,' said Valentine. They had run out of time already.

'And . . . it sounds daft, but . . . I could tell it was *feeling* for something. For me.'

'Can you see it now?' he asked, glancing round anxiously.

She shook her head. 'I don't think so. Though sometimes I think I do, from the corner of my eye . . . and . . . there's something else.'

'What is it?'

'It's embarrassing.'

'Oh?'

She lowered her voice to a whisper, even though nobody could possibly hear them. 'I think I'm starting to . . . go off.'

'Huh?'

'You know . . . go bad. Spoil. Rot.' Her expression was one of utter disgust.

Now she had said it, he could see it too. She wasn't just pale – she was waxy. Her eyes were more sunken than before, causing heavy shadows on her face, skull-like. Her lips were nearly as white as her skin and dry and cracked. Sure enough, the process of decomposition was starting.

DECOMPOSITION

Dee-comp-oh-SI-shun

The decay of organic matter after death, the natural process of a body returning to the earth.

A useful process to prevent an excess of corpses lying about.

Less convenient for a body still in use.

'That's enough – no need to stare.' She turned away impatiently. 'Anyway, the important thing is, I believe you now, about everything, and I don't want the Never to get my soul, so, yank it out and take me down to your library, or whatever.'

She clenched her jaw and stood straight, chin up.

Valentine took a deep, slow breath, and moved closer to her, until they were almost nose to nose. 'I hate this,' he said. 'I want you to stay with me.'

'Me too,' said Philomena.

'If there was any other way . . .' He reached towards her face.

'Wait!'

He withdrew his hand, sharply.

Philomena produced the book from her apron pocket and shoved it against Valentine's chest. 'Here. Take this. I suppose you'll need to put it back in the library when this is over.'

He nodded and tucked it carefully into his cloak.

'I'm ready. Is it going to hurt?' There was a slight shake in Philomena's voice. She shut her eyes.

'No,' said Valentine, but he was hurting inside. *Mustn't think about it. Just get it done.* He sought the spot an inch above her skin where her honey-coloured soul should lie, but he couldn't feel it. He moved a little closer, expecting the pressure of the air to change, but . . . nothing. 'Hmm.'

'What's wrong?'

'Nothing, except . . .' It had definitely been there before – he had felt it when she hugged him. He put his fingers directly on her face now – the skin seemed tighter than it used to be. 'You're cold.'

Cold was a bad sign.

'That's what happens to dead things,' she replied.

But – ah, *there* – her soul, a flicker of it, thin as silk, right against the skin itself. Still warm. Barely.

'Here goes,' he said. He tenderly pinched Philomena's soul between finger and thumb, but he couldn't get a grip. He tried again. 'Wait. One second.' Valentine examined her cheekbones, her jaw, the lobes of her ears, searching for somewhere he might get a better grasp. Finally, he thought he had it, on the front of her neck just beneath her chin. He tugged.

The soul wouldn't come out.

'What's taking so long?' Philomena opened one eye. 'Hurry up, before the Never gets here!'

'I'm trying,' he said. 'But it won't budge. We need help. But Death is on a collection, and I don't know where, or when he'll be back. What do we do now?'

'I don't know! How would I know anyone who could help? Nobody even remembers I exist!'

'Hush a second.'

'What?'

'Wait, I'm thinking.' Perhaps they did know someone who could help. All the pieces fell into place in his head.

'What was it the midwife told you to call her?'

'Mother Mercy?'

Mother Mercy.

Mother Misery.

'She's the one. Come on. We need to find her.'

He ran towards the cemetery gate. Philomena was right behind him. Captain Bones, sensing the excitement, lolloped along at their heels.

'Not you, dog,' Valentine panted. 'Stay here, boy.'

He unlocked the gate and stepped through on to the bustling cobbled streets. Captain Bones jumped through behind them. He landed, turned two full circles and growled at the enchanted gate suspiciously.

'Go on, into the graveyard,' said Valentine. 'I need to lock up.'

But the dog wouldn't budge, digging his paws into the dirt when Valentine tried to push him back inside.

'Fine,' he said, slamming the gate shut. 'Only because we don't have time. Stay close, all right?'

Bones barked in eager agreement.

Philomena was standing statue-still, mouth open.

'What's up?' said Valentine. 'We need to move.'

'Where are all the people?' she said.

Valentine saw two boys washing windows. A little girl

playing with a black-and-white cat. A man and woman arm-in-arm.

'What do you mean?'

'There's nobody here – where is everyone?'

Valentine frowned. He stepped in front of her and waved his hand in her face. 'How many fingers am I holding up?'

'Three,' she said. 'It's not my eyes.'

Her eyes *were* a little different, though, less shiny, a slight milkiness over the brown of her irises.

'But you don't see anyone? That girl, over there with the cat?' He pointed.

'No. No girl. No cat.'

'The man over there by the graves?'

'There's nobody there, Valentine.'

'What *can* you see?'

'I see you, the gate, the buildings. That's it.'

'Come on!' He grabbed her by the arm and pulled her along as he started to run.

'Valentine! Wait!' She yanked her arm away. 'On my own, they're all gone, but –' she grabbed hold of him again – 'now it's back to normal. I can see them when we're touching!'

'And I can see the Never,' said Valentine.

It *was* coming. Just a hint of it, flowing over the rooftops, sniffing for their scent like a dog hunting a rabbit.

They set off running once again, Valentine stopping briefly to scoop up Captain Bones, who was struggling to keep up with them. They reached Mercy's door and burst through it, straight into the house, and found her hunched over a table, writing in a large, heavy-looking book.

'I can still see her,' said Philomena. 'She's different.'

'Can I help you?' the old woman said, without glancing up.

'It's me. Death's apprentice.' Valentine was panting.

'I am aware,' she said. 'Who are you here for, then? It can't be me.'

'Because you can't die, can you, Mother Misery?'

This made her set down her pen and give Valentine her full attention.

'I 'ent been *her* for many a century.'

Captain Bones had smelled something tasty bubbling away over the fire and was trying to wriggle out of Valentine's arms to investigate.

'We need your help, please.'

'Who is *we*?'

'Oh.' Valentine had forgotten for a moment that she wouldn't see Philomena. 'Mena, hold her hand.'

Philomena sat down on the bench seat beside the old woman and clasped one gnarled old claw in both of her hands. 'Mother Mercy,' she said. 'I'm Philomena, remember?'

A shadow of recognition passed over Mercy's face before a suspicious glare settled in and pointed itself at Valentine. 'What's going on here?'

He shook his head with frustration. 'Philomena was your

apprentice, and I was supposed to take her soul, but I saved her instead.'

'Ohhhhhh, I see.' She nodded wisely as though this sort of thing happened to her all the time.

'But now the Never is after her and I can't get her soul out.'

'Slow down, son.' Mercy withdrew her hands, laced her fingers together and rested her chin on them. 'What do you need?'

'What happened to stop you from dying, so we can do that for Philomena?'

'For who?'

Philomena groaned and put her hand on Mercy's shoulder. 'I'm Philomena.'

'Of course you are. Stop fading in and out of reality. It's confusing.'

The dog yapped, then buried his face in a bowl on the floor.

'Can you save her from the Never? Make it so she's alive properly again?'

'I'm human. I don't have powers over life and death.'

Valentine looked down at Mercy's table and the work they had interrupted – some sort of diary, perhaps, with complicated diagrams and notes. The old woman noticed his gaze and snapped the book shut, defensively. But Valentine was more interested in what she was writing with.

'Then why hasn't the Never eaten you?' said Philomena.

'Because the Never only fixes mistakes. I'm not a mistake.

240

It was all done officially.'

'Your book,' said Valentine. 'Did he write something in your book? Is that how it's done?' He set Philomena's book on the table.

The woman nodded. 'But you can't—'

He snatched up Mother Mercy's quill pen and dipped it clumsily into the inkwell, thick drips of black ink splattering on to the table.

'Rude!' said Mother Mercy.

Valentine flipped the book to the last page.

'It won't work,' said Mercy.

Philomena leaned over the table to watch as Valentine set the nib on to the page and scribbled out the word 'died'. The ink shrank back and pooled into droplets on the surface, as though he were trying to draw on glass. He tried again. He scratched and scratched over that spot. Still the ink wouldn't seep into the paper. Next, he tried to write the word 'lived' over the top of it – again it wouldn't stick, and as soon as he moved the book, the teardrops of ink simply slid off.

'Why can't I do it?' Valentine half yelled with frustration.

'Because it's a life book! You're not writing words. You're writing events. Reality. Experience. Of course normal ink doesn't work.' Mother Mercy wiped the ink spots from

241

the table with the corner of a rag. 'You need Permanent Ink.'

'What's that?' said Philomena.

'Oh, the proper stuff that lasts for ever. It's made of void, and time, and who knows what else, whereas this ink . . .'

Philomena looked to Valentine. 'So if we can get the right ink . . . ?'

Mother Mercy carefully closed the lid of the inkwell. 'This is made of oak galls and rusty nails and urine.'

'Ugh!' Valentine quickly dropped the pen and wiped his fingers on his cloak.

'Magic ink,' said Philomena. 'Death must have it.'

'Nay, child, not any more. They took it away from him, after the deal he made with yours truly.'

'Where is it, then?' said Valentine, impatiently. If all they had to do was find some special ink, they had a shot.

The woman shrugged. 'Locked away deep in the who-knows-where. You'd need to ask Death. What has he said about all this business?'

'He doesn't know,' said Valentine. 'I thought I could fix it without him finding out.'

She sighed heavily and stood up. 'Hop to it, then.'

'You'll help us?'

'Us?' said Mercy. 'Who's us? You and the dog?'

Philomena resumed contact.

'Me and Philomena,' said Valentine.

'Yes, obviously you and Philomena,' said Mercy. 'I'm not a

fool. First things first, we need to tell Death.'

'I'm not sure—'

'Bit late for not sure, boy. If there's anything to be done – and I'm not saying there is, mind – you won't do it without him on board.'

'He went on a collection.'

'Then we'll go to him,' said Mercy.

'But I don't know where he is.'

She bustled outside, mumbling something under her breath about apprentices these days having no common sense. 'Summon the horse.'

He put two fingers in his mouth the way he saw Death do it, and blew, but no sound came out. He tried again, spraying his knuckles with spit but not managing to whistle.

'Pathetic,' said Mercy. She whistled herself, and a moment later the rumbling of Gytrash's great hoofs began.

'We'll need something to stand on to get on his back,' said Valentine.

'My tree,' said Mercy, opening the gate. The great tree in her garden – so old and strong it had lifted the pavement and sent cracks through the wall with its roots – waited with conveniently placed branches.

'Hold on,' said Valentine. 'Is that the apple tree you trapped Death in?'

'Pear tree!' Mercy snapped. 'You don't need to worry. That enchantment wore off years ago.'

Valentine hesitated – this could be a trap. If they climbed up now and got stuck, then everything was over. 'I don't think—'

'No time to think, Valentine,' said Philomena.

She touched his arm and pointed upwards. Sure enough, the Never was approaching. It was still oozing, creeping, as though it hadn't spotted her yet, but he could hear the rushing of air and sense the swelling iciness. *It was closing in.*

He nodded. Better to try something than nothing. He set Captain Bones down in the yard, hoisted himself up into the tree and offered a hand to Philomena. Mercy refused his help and clambered up herself with impressive agility for a woman of several hundred years. Bones scrabbled and scratched at the trunk.

'Don't you let that smelly little creature hurt my tree, Valentine Crow,' said Mercy sternly. 'You know what happens to people who mess with my tree.'

He reached down and Captain Bones jumped into his arms. 'You've got to behave, though, understood?' The dog licked his face.

Gytrash came to a sudden halt in front of them, snorting powerfully through his giant nostrils, then helpfully brought himself over to the side of the tree.

Valentine carefully climbed from pear tree to horse with Captain Bones awkwardly tucked under his cloak. Philomena came next; then at her back, Mother Mercy.

Valentine took two handfuls of Gytrash's mane, hoping the dog wouldn't slip out from his cloak with all the wriggling and fall off. 'Is everyone holding tight? Gytrash, take us to Death.'

Wearing a Wooden Overcoat

This ride was even more terrifying than Valentine had remembered. Without Death there, he wasn't at all sure that he could keep his grip, and he suspected Gytrash knew it. They all fell silent as the world dissolved away and they plunged through the darkness on the otherworldly beast. Gytrash was swift, and it was only minutes before his vast hoofs clattered down on to solid ground. They emerged from the void in one piece, and the creature came to his usual jarring halt.

'Good, um, horse,' said Valentine, half sliding, half falling down from Gytrash's back, doing his best not to drop Captain Bones. Philomena copied his technique while Mercy brought both feet together and jumped, landing with surprising grace.

Valentine didn't recognize the village they'd arrived in. A

pub squatted on one corner of a street of higgledy-piggledy houses, and the buildings opened out into a churchyard on the other. It was brighter and more open than London, and the air smelled sweet in comparison. He shaded his eyes with his hand and looked around for Death.

'If he's in one of these houses, how will we find him?'

Captain Bones yelped excitedly from under Valentine's arm.

'Hush, you,' said Valentine. 'Your breath stinks.'

Bones yapped again, snuffling at Valentine's cheek with his wet nose.

The moment he set him down, the dog raced towards the churchyard. A moment later he returned, circled the three of them, then pushed through Valentine's legs, almost knocking him over, before trotting off in the same direction.

'He's telling you to follow him,' said Philomena.

As they reached the lychgate of the church, they spotted a small crowd gathered alongside an open grave. It didn't look like a funeral – the people wore work clothes, and there was no sign of the priest.

'That's promising,' said Mercy, and began stumping towards them.

'What?' said Philomena. 'I can't see anything.'

There was no sign of Death either.

'Stay with Mercy,' said Valentine, 'so you don't bump into anyone.'

He ran up the sloping grass, overtaking Bones, and reached

the graveside first. As usual, none of the living people paid him any attention. Toes on the edge of the hole, he peered down into the grave.

It was a long way down. Twenty coffins deep at least. A ladder, long and rickety, leaned up against the inside of the hole, and on both sides stacks of coffins were visible here and there from the neighbouring graves, barely a spoonful of dirt separating each one from their neighbours.

'Valentine!' said Death, who was standing at the bottom of the hole. 'I told you not to come to this one. Don't come down here, whatever you do. Poisonous gas. That's what all this is about.' He gestured to his feet, where three bodies already lay – not neatly laid out in coffins and shrouds but slumped together in a pile.

'Can you come up, then?' stage-whispered Valentine. He glanced nervously over his shoulder.

'I shall get them out,' said a youngish man, removing his cap and rolling up his sleeves. A ripple of approval passed through the people standing by the graves.

'It isn't safe,' said an older man in smart clothes. 'You'll end up the same way.'

'I need your help,' Valentine hissed down to Death. 'It's important.'

'Give me –' he checked the watch – 'about one more minute. Nearly finished here.'

'They might be alive down there,' said the first man.

'They're not,' called Death from down below.

'If we can get them out, we might save them yet.'

'Is the Never here?' Valentine called to Mercy and Philomena, who were steadily making their way towards him arm-in-arm.

Philomena shook her head. 'I don't think it's caught up with us yet.'

That was something, at least. They could outrun it. Although they couldn't keep running for ever.

The youngest man at the graveside had tied a rope round his waist and handed the end of the rope to the nearest onlooker. 'Keep hold of this between you. If I should faint, you can pull me back up, quickly.'

'Will you hurry up and die, please?' muttered Valentine. 'This is an emergency!'

The man descended the ladder, clearly not noticing that he was moving towards Death. 'Perfectly safe,' he called up.

The very next second, he swooned. His limbs went limp and he fell off the ladder. The rope went taut and caught him barely two feet above the pile of corpses.

'Pull!' shouted a man up top.

'Death,' hissed Valentine, 'I've got a huge problem.'

'Be with you in a moment,' said Death as the unconscious man was lifted jerkily up towards the mouth of the grave.

He was almost at the top when the knot, clumsily tied, gave way. The rope unravelled round the unfortunate man, and he fell straight back down. Death swiftly snatched away his soul half a second before the body landed and placed it carefully into a pocket. 'Idiots,' he muttered and began to climb out.

The people surrounding the grave were shouting and panicking and arguing, but Valentine ignored them – he had his own tragedy to focus on.

Death froze on the second step and pointed at Mercy and Philomena. 'What are *they* doing here?'

He climbed out of the pit and wiped soil-stained hands on his cloak.

'Come to think of it, what are *you* doing here?'

'I made a mistake,' said Valentine. 'I need your help.'

'We can't talk out here.' Death pointed towards a tool shed behind the church and began striding towards it. 'The gravedigger's hut. He won't be needing it any more.'

The shed was even smaller than the mausoleum. There was only one stool, which Mercy took. Valentine, Philomena and Captain Bones squeezed into the corner, while Death's vast greasy wings took up most of the remaining space. Valentine was sure he was staying large on purpose, to show his disapproval.

'You prevented the accident?' Death said with folded arms.

'I thought it was a good idea.'

'And you didn't take the soul.'

'Right.' Valentine couldn't look directly at him.

'And you lied to me about it.'

'I didn't lie,' Valentine said, weakly. 'I just didn't tell you.'

'That's lying! Secrets are just quiet lies. You kept this hidden from me, *on purpose?*'

Valentine nodded. Philomena squeezed his hand. Mother Mercy wasn't troubled by the uncomfortable tension – she was tucking into the gravedigger's lunch of cheese and fruitcake.

'No use wasting it,' she mumbled to herself. Captain Bones sat up very straight at her feet, hoping for scraps.

'And then you go behind my back, to *this* woman, the bane of my existence, my not-so-mortal enemy?'

'I didn't know where you were,' said Valentine. 'And I thought you were friends.'

'We are both,' he said. 'Depending on the circumstances.'

'We thought she would know how to make me alive again,' said Philomena. 'Because you let her live.'

'Firstly –' Death raised a finger – 'I did not *let* her live; she blackmailed me. And secondly, it isn't possible.'

'But the book—' Valentine objected. 'We've got her book. Can't you just write in it, the way you did with Mother Mercy?'

'How many times, Valentine? I can't. And I wouldn't even if I could. There are rules. Why didn't you take her soul once you realized what was happening?'

'Whose soul?' said Mother Mercy with her mouth full.

'Her soul!' Death pointed to Philomena, exasperated.

251

'Who else could we possibly be talking about?'

'She can't see Philomena unless they're touching. Or remember her,' explained Valentine. 'Since the missed death-time.'

'Remember who?' said Mercy.

'That's going to get annoying,' said Death.

'He tried to take my soul, in the end,' interrupted Philomena, 'but it wouldn't come away. Valentine said it's as though it isn't loose any more.'

'Come here.'

She took two nervous steps towards Death. She cringed as his long, skeletal fingers crept to her face.

'Are you going to do it now?' said Philomena, twisting her apron in her trembling hands.

'Don't!' begged Valentine. 'Please, let her live.'

'I can't,' said Death. 'But, for now I'm just feeling for her soul. It's . . . ahhh, yes, there it is. Hmmm. It's cooling.'

'Take it, then,' said Philomena. 'Go on. Don't let the Never get me.'

Death nodded. 'Sensible choice.'

Valentine covered his eyes. He couldn't bear to see the moment when the spark left Philomena's body and she fell to the ground.

The silence stretched out. All he could hear was the steady wet munching of Mercy eating with her mouth open, and the hopeful panting of Captain Bones.

'Oh dear,' said Death at last. 'It's completely stuck.'

Valentine looked up again.

'What does that mean?' said Philomena.

'Too late. I can't get your soul out now.'

'Whose soul?' said Mercy.

Philomena made a frustrated whimper and stepped back to put her hand on Mercy's shoulder.

'Oh, your soul,' said Mercy, nodding sagely.

'But you're Death!' said Valentine. 'If you can't do it, then . . . then what?'

'Then the Never will.'

'No!' said Valentine. 'That's not fair! Why does she have to go? Why did she have to die in the first place?'

'Everybody has to die, Valentine; that's how it goes.'

'I hate it. I hate it, and I hate you and I hate this whole stupid system.'

'*Now* you see my point,' said Mercy.

'Take me back to the hospital, then. I won't be your apprentice any more.'

'You're taking it too personally,' said Death. 'This is how things go sometimes. You have to accept it.'

'I won't!' said Valentine. 'She didn't do anything wrong; I did! And you did, by bringing me into this in the first place. Please! Fix it!'

Now Death folded in his wings and made himself a little smaller. 'I'm not as powerful as you think.' He sighed. 'I used to be. They let me make decisions, little adjustments, a few extra lines at the end of a book.'

'So can't you—?'

Death stopped him. 'The whole Mother Misery thing was a disaster. So many people missing their death times. Head office was furious. Furious that I'd let everything get in such a mess, and even more furious that I'd rewarded her bad behaviour.'

'Get to the point, you old fool,' said Mercy. 'This child doesn't have time to waste.'

'Anyway, everything changed. They divided us up, the reapers, gave us our own sections of the world and time. Wouldn't let me have apprentices any more. They took away my power to adjust people's lifespans completely. I can't do it now. Not even by a day or two.'

'Why didn't the Never come and take all the souls when you were trapped?' asked Philomena.

'The Never didn't do that, back then. It was kept contained. Only fed on the very worst souls. Kept on a very short leash.'

'So why is it roaming free now?' asked Valentine.

Death looked distinctly uncomfortable for a minute, then awkwardly cleared his throat.

'After all that business with the tree, they made the Never free-range . . . to prevent the universe getting out of balance again.'

'Can it be put back? The Never?'

Death stared at the floor. 'No. It was a one-way thing. Think about it. How do you contain nothingness?'

A momentary silence descended on the gravedigger's hut. Philomena's chin dropped and her shoulders slumped, drained of all hope.

'No,' said Valentine.

'No what?' said Death.

'No, I don't accept this. I don't care about any of that stuff. There has to be something we can do.' Philomena met his eye, and it spurred him on. 'You wrote in Mother Mercy's book with Permanent Ink, yes?'

'That he did, son.' Mercy's words were muffled as she picked a piece of raisin out of her teeth.

'I don't have that any more. They took it away to destroy it.'

'They destroyed it?!' Philomena wailed.

'No,' said Death. 'They tried to destroy it, but they couldn't. It's permanent. It can't be destroyed.'

Valentine growled with irritation. 'Where is it, then?'

'Nowhere we can reach it. Deep in the back rooms of the library. You can't even get into the room without approval from the Higher-Ups.'

'But it's there. It exists. We can try, right?'

Death fidgeted. He rubbed the back of his head. 'Possibly ... It'll never work. I suppose . . . there might be something, but . . .'

'Please?' said Valentine.

'Please?' said Philomena.

'Yip,' yipped Captain Bones.

'But I can't simply say, hey, would you mind quickly extending the lifetime of this random girl—'

'Hey!'

'—because my illegal apprentice let his squishy *human* brain get in the way of doing his job, and then we didn't fix it in time and, oopsie-daisy, here comes the Never.'

'Why not?' Philomena folded her arms.

'Because I am already under inspection and I am *this close* –' he indicated with his fingers barely a hair's breadth apart – 'to being demoted again, and then what? Hmmm? No more cosy reaping souls for me – I'll be scraping dead cats off the pavement for the rest of eternity!'

'What are you talking about?' said Philomena.

'And did you think about this, Valentine?' said Death, ignoring Philomena entirely. 'It's not just me. What do you think will happen to you if they find out you're my human apprentice? Do you think they'll let you back out into the world, now that you've seen the Always and the Never?'

Valentine went cold. 'What *will* happen to me?!'

'I don't know. But I think there's a small chance that they might see this whole thing . . . *you* . . . as . . . a mistake.'

Valentine stepped back in shock. Captain Bones placed himself between his master and Death and growled up at the reaper protectively. 'Why would you take me as an apprentice at all, then? Why would you do this to me?'

'Because it wasn't supposed to turn out this way. We were going to be a huge success and *then* I would reveal the truth and they'd promote me and give me my old powers back and—'

'This is all about you, then?' asked Valentine, pointedly. 'Who cares what happens to us mere mortals, as long as you get your rewards? Is that how it is?'

Mother Mercy rocked back in her seat. 'You tell him, boy.'

'Valentine,' said Death, in a measured, calm tone, like someone who was trying very hard to be reasonable but finding it extremely difficult. 'May I speak to you outside for a moment? Alone?'

Valentine nodded reluctantly. They stepped out of the gravedigger's hut and Death closed the door firmly. Across the graveyard, people were still pacing around the open grave and having animated conversations about what to do next.

'I know it's hard when things go wrong, but the solution is very simple,' said Death. 'We don't even have to do anything. Let the Never take her. Get back to work. Carry on as if nothing happened. Nobody needs to know.'

'We can't do that to Philomena!'

'Is non-existence really so bad?' said Death. 'She won't be hurting or scared.'

'But she'll be gone. She'll miss out on all those other lives she's supposed to have. And the Always.'

'But is it worth risking *your* soul over, Valentine?'

'It is.' Understanding trickled down the back of his neck like rainwater. 'Because she's my kindred spirit.'

That was it. That was why he was drawn to her. That was what got in the way of him putting things right, even when he knew what he had to do. How could anyone expect him to take the soul of his own kindred spirit? Their souls belonged together.

'Oh,' said Death. 'All right, then.'

'All right?'

'All right, then.' Death held Valentine's gaze for an unbearably long moment. And then he winked.

Valentine lunged at Death and hugged him, an odd, uncomfortable hug, since there was very little of Death to embrace, only bones, fabric and ginormous greasy feathers. The shed door slammed open, and Philomena and Mercy practically fell out of it, arms linked, with Captain Bones shoving his way past their ankles.

'We were listening,' said Philomena.

'Of course you were,' said Death. 'To the library, then. Oh boy, I am not looking forward to this.'

'Can we go right now, please?' said Philomena. 'Because I can see the Never.'

On Futility

To say that an action is futile, is
to say that no matter how hard you
try, you are doomed to fail.

To save Philomena, Valentine and his
companions must descend into the liminal
space between life and death, then
navigate through a vast maze of corridors,
without being noticed, while outrunning
the relentless emptiness of the Never,
and convince an eternal being to allow an
exception to the rules of the universe.
The odds against them
are overwhelming.

Their situation is futile.

At the Pearly Gates

Death whistled for Gytrash. The monstrous horse effortlessly leaped the churchyard walls and crossed the space in three seconds, his hoofs dashing alarmingly close to the people by the graveside, who of course took no notice of him at all.

'Up we get then.' Death lifted Philomena up first.

Gytrash snorted.

'Yes, all of us. You're a hell horse – you can manage a skeleton, two children and an old woman.'

Bones yapped and Valentine scooped him into his cloak pocket.

'And a dog,' added Death.

Death swung up himself, sitting in front of Philomena, then hauled Valentine and Captain Bones in front of him.

He beckoned to Mercy.

'Come on, you wretched woman,' said Death. 'She doesn't have long.'

'Who doesn't?' said Mercy.

Death groaned. 'One moment, children, sorry. Mercy, come closer. Closer.' He patted down his cloak then pulled something from a deep pocket. 'One more step, that's it.'

Once Mercy was within arm's reach of Gytrash, Death leaned down towards her and quickly blew a handful of dust directly into Mercy's eyes. She recoiled immediately, rubbing her face with her sleeve.

'What did you do that for, you hideous—!' She spat and blinked hard.

'Time dust,' said Death to the children. 'She should be able to see you now, Philomena. At least until it all comes out of her eyes.'

'Of course I can see Philomena!' Mercy snapped. 'What are we waiting for?'

Death put out his arms to help her up. 'We're waiting for you, you daft harpy!'

'I will not have you lifting me up like a child!' She wagged her finger at Death. 'I will do this the *ladylike* way.' She rolled up her sleeves. 'By climbing a tree.'

She selected a suitable oak and dragged herself up. There was a fair bit of puffing and panting, and Valentine didn't think it strictly counted as ladylike, but it was impressive, nonetheless. Mother Mercy put her arms round Philomena to grab hold of Death's cloak. Philomena put her arms round Death and held on to Valentine. Then Gytrash was lumbering, galloping, thundering, up, and away.

They were all holding on to each other, and that meant that all of them could sense the Never.

A chill descended, as though the heat was being stolen from their bodies, and the sky was beginning to darken. It was closer now. Valentine could tell. Philomena was shaking – or somebody was – with their bodies pressed together, it was hard to tell who. Gytrash picked up pace. With a bound, he was over the churchyard wall, but the clunk of landing never happened – they were riding through the blackness and when they emerged in the safety of their own graveyard, the Never was nowhere to be seen.

'Phew,' said Valentine.

'It has your scent now, Philomena,' said Death. 'And your soul is growing colder by the minute. It won't be long before it finds us again. Into the mausoleum.'

He strode directly through the closed wooden door, leaving Valentine to fumble for his key and let the others inside. By the time he'd done that, Death had already dragged open the slab in the floor.

Valentine and Philomena went inside, but Mercy hesitated on the threshold.

'You must be curious, after all this time,' said Death

provokingly.

'I thought living humans weren't allowed in the library.'

'I think we're past worrying about the rules now.'

Mercy grunted her assent and stumped over to the top step. 'But don't get any funny ideas. Our agreement still stands. No dying for me.'

'Understood,' said Death.

'I'm scared,' whispered Philomena as they made their way down the dark staircase.

'Me too,' said Valentine. 'But you'll feel better once we reach the library. It has that effect.'

'About that,' said Death. 'The library might be a problem for us.'

'Why?' said Philomena.

'The Never is on your case, now, and the Never and the Always don't mix.'

'What does that mean?' said Valentine.

'It means we need to keep Philomena moving. The Always and the Never, they're two opposite energies. They repel each other. If they get too close, problems happen. Things get weird. Mistakes. That's why we have the vacant room, Valentine. So the Never *doesn't* come hunting for them in the library.'

Valentine's heart was pounding. His whole body was preparing to run, or to fight, but it wasn't that sort of danger they were facing. He glanced at Philomena. They had to save her. But how?

At the bottom of the steps, Valentine opened the door to the library, and they all went through.

Philomena gasped.

'Hm,' said Mercy. 'Not too bad.'

'It's the most beautiful thing I've ever seen,' said Philomena. 'I could stay here for ever.'

'No, you can't,' said Death, holding the back of her arm in his bony grasp. 'Remember? The Never? Bad things?'

'Bad things,' said Philomena, dreamily, then snapped to her senses. 'Bad things. Yes.'

'Listen, all of you,' said Death.

Valentine, Philomena and Mercy huddled close, as Death spoke in a low voice and outlined his plan.

'. . . I need to scout things out. And you need to stay here.'

'Right,' said Valentine. 'We can do that.'

'Except,' said Death, 'I also need you to not stay here.'

'What?' said Valentine.

'Keep moving.'

Death turned and swished away, striding towards the spot with the hidden bookcase doorway.

'Come back!' Philomena shouted after him. 'Where do we go?'

'I know,' said Valentine, thinking on his feet. 'Come on.'

He took Philomena's hand and ran over to one of the doorways.

'Mother Mercy, are you coming?' he called back, holding

the door open with his foot.

'I'll slow you down.' She waved them away. 'You go, boy. Save your souls.'

Valentine and Philomena rushed through the doorway with the long, carved tunnels and let the door bang closed behind them.

A moment of quiet. A deep breath. Now what?

'Where are we?' asked Philomena. 'It's warm.'

But Philomena was cold. Cold to the touch and getting colder. They didn't have much time left. He hoped Death knew what he was doing.

'I have no idea,' said Valentine. 'Somewhere far, far away from London. And hopefully that means far, far away from the Never.'

Philomena looked relieved, but only for a moment. 'But it's going to find us here, too.'

'Then we go through a different door. We keep running.'

He wondered whether they could do that for ever. Just him and Philomena, moving from one corner of the earth to another for a few hours of safety before the Never caught up with them. Maybe that's what they'd have to do if they failed to make things right.

Philomena rested her head on his shoulder.

'Thank you,' she said.

'For what?' asked Valentine. As far as he could tell, he'd done nothing but make things worse for Philomena.

'For trying,' she said. 'No one has ever cared enough to try this hard for me before.' It was so quiet, and so still, and they were together, and this was how things were meant to feel, he was sure of it.

But not yet. A cold breeze snaked its way around them, cutting through the hot, stuffy air in the tunnels. A coldness that didn't belong in this place.

'I think it's coming,' said Valentine.

'Valentine!' Philomena's voice was fearful. 'It's here.'

'Already?' This was too fast. It was faster every time it appeared. How long could they keep it at bay?

Sure enough, the black tendrils of nothing were slithering into the end of the corridor, and the ground beneath their feet was shuddering and trembling.

They tumbled back through the door and into the library.

'Which way next?' said Philomena.

'Any. This one.'

They raced across the floor.

This was the door that led to the riverbank. They saw no sign of the Never – not yet.

It was night-time here, but beneath them ten thousand

candles illuminated the shores, and the air was alive with sweet incense and the distant tones of unfamiliar music. To catch their breath, they sat on steps over the glittering water. The great bonfires burning on the other bank sent up such heat that the air itself bent and swayed, dreamlike and eerie.

'Where are we?' asked Philomena after a moment. 'It's beautiful.'

'I don't know.'

'There's so much of the world we haven't seen yet.' Her eyes were milky. Even in the warm orange light of the flames, Valentine could tell that her skin was getting paler, her lips taking on a bluish tinge.

The ground beneath them shuddered. They leaped to their feet.

'It's there.' Philomena pointed across the river where a tendril of non-existence was unfurling, blocking out the tiny droplets of light from row after row of candles.

She was ahead of Valentine this time. She burst through the door and kept running full tilt across the library to the door on the opposite side. Heaving it open, she flung herself through and Valentine was only

half a second behind.

Salty air. The ocean. The lighthouse.

It was lighter here. The seas were calmer than the last time Valentine found himself balancing on these slippery, sharp rocks, but they pressed themselves back against the towering building all the same. The water churned and foamed as each wave broke against the tiny, stony island.

'It might take longer to find us here, out on the water,' said Valentine. He didn't believe it. Which direction would it come from? They were completely exposed. What if it was sneaking up behind them, on the other side of the lighthouse?

'Valentine,' said Philomena, her eyes scanning the empty horizon. 'One of the doors in the library goes to the Always, right?'

'Yes.' They had to shout over the relentless noise of wind and waves.

'What happens if I walk straight into the Always like this? Still with my body?'

'I don't know,' said Valentine. 'Death told me if I go too close, my soul might be sucked out of my body, so I suppose . . .'

'That's what we need to do, then, isn't it?'

'Is it?'

'Take me there. Let it suck my soul out. Even if Death can't get the soul loose, maybe the Always will. It's better than the Never, isn't it? It's better than you ending up in the Never too, and Death being in trouble and all of that?'

'But we might still be able to save you,' said Valentine. 'Shouldn't we try?'

'I don't know if we have any trying left.'

'I don't want you to go,' said Valentine. 'I'll miss you.'

'But it won't be for ever, will it? Kindred spirits, right?'

He hesitated. He couldn't bear that solution. 'But Death is helping us now – he might be back with the answer any moment, and if we give up—'

'Is he?' said Philomena. Her teeth were chattering now, from the weather and the fear and the cooling of her soul. 'We don't know where he's really gone, or if he's coming back for us.'

It hit him, with more force than a tidal wave, how ridiculous it was to think that they could count on Death for help. Valentine had become so used to Death's presence, his gifts, his jokes . . . he'd started to think of Death as a friend. But he was Death. Why would he risk himself to save two mortal children? They were specks of dust to him.

Philomena squeezed Valentine's hand. 'Let's do it now, before we run out of time for good.'

Something changed. The wind and the water were retreating. The sea level sank, exposing the layers of slime-and-seaweed-covered granite beneath the lighthouse, retreating on all sides, rolling back towards the horizon. With a lurch, Valentine understood that the Never had found them already, circling them, billowing like filthy smoke over the horizon in all directions.

'Yes,' said Valentine. 'Let's go.'

Back in the library, they approached the doorway to the Always. Valentine tried to open it, but it wouldn't budge.

'Because it's not your time, I suppose,' said Philomena. She was radiating calm. Incredibly calm, considering she had faced worse truths than Valentine, and had less time to get used to it. Tranquility began to wash over him too. Taking Philomena to the Always really was the best thing, after all. Why hadn't they done this to begin with?

She turned the handle.

It wouldn't open for her, either.

She tugged on it. Nothing. It didn't budge at all.

'Excuse me!' she called to the nearest librarian. 'I can't get the door open.'

'Then you haven't answered your soul's question yet,' said the librarian.

'I don't have time for that,' she said. 'I need to go, now.'

'Please open it,' said Valentine. 'It's an emergency.'

'Valentine Crow,' said the librarian. 'We cannot change the workings of the library. It is what it is.'

Valentine had to lean against the door to steady himself. He had only just prepared himself to say goodbye to Philomena and now they were thwarted again. Thwarted by pointless rules that made no sense at all.

There was a booming sound and the whole library shook. In several places books were knocked from shelves, scattering across the floor. Even the librarians looked startled.

'What was that?' asked Philomena, as the whole room rocked to one side and then righted itself. She clutched Valentine's sleeve to steady herself.

Then, thin wisps of the Never began seeping down from the ceiling high above.

'Run!' yelled Valentine, and they dashed through the next doorway, panting and terrified.

It was pitch-black inside.

'We can't stay here,' said Valentine. 'We might not see the Never until it's too late.' He opened the door a crack. All was clear in the library – no smoky blackness, no sudden movements. The librarians were calmly replacing the books.

'Are you ready? We have to move fast, straight to another door.'

'Ready,' said Philomena. They held tight to one another as they dashed into the next entrance.

Before the door was even closed, there was a blinding

flash of silver-white lightning and a stinging spray of freezing, salty water. They were back at the lighthouse. Valentine could hardly catch his breath. The sky above was dark, with flashes of lightning and rolls of thunder. The waves beat at the desolate rock relentlessly.

'Hold on to something,' cried out Philomena, but there was nothing to hold on to. They pressed their backs against the lighthouse wall, but the water surged and threatened to cast them off into the seething depths with every wave.

'We haven't tried all the other doors yet,' said Valentine desperately. 'There's a cave somewhere, I think. We can hide there.'

He opened the door once again and returned to the library, but this time things were not calm.

'There!' One of the librarians pointed in his direction. 'Get them out of here!'

'That way,' said Valentine. 'We need to keep moving until Death comes back for us.'

'Is that where Death went? Through there?' Philomena pointed to a bookcase standing askew, with barely a sliver of light visible behind it. It was the same one they'd used to get to the vacant room – Death must have left the doorway open.

'We can't, Philomena. They'll catch us.'

'They might catch us here, too.'

And without another word, they raced for the doorway.

On the Other Side

'Is this it?' asked Philomena, as Valentine closed the door behind them. Not that closed doors made much difference, any more.

'It?' he said, breathlessly.

'All this way to the end of everything and it's a bunch of grey walls? That's disappointing.'

'Uh huh,' said Valentine. He was beyond caring about such things now. He ran down the corridor, trying to find a balance between fast and quiet. They turned a corner, and then another – they passed the vacant room, and Valentine turned his face away.

A minute later, though, they reached a fork in the path.

'Which way do we go?' said Philomena.

'I don't know,' said Valentine. 'I don't even know what

we're searching for, or what we'll do when we find it.'

They froze helplessly.

In desperation, Valentine remembered his pocket watch. He took it out, opened it and tapped on the glass, hoping for a sign.

'I know it's not what you're meant to do,' he said. 'But is there any chance . . . ?'

The watch did nothing. The floor rumbled.

'It's coming,' said Philomena. 'Pick one.'

They darted down the right-hand path. Behind them, the Never lurched into view, more substantial now, banging clumsily against the wall. They kept running. A short while later the corridor opened up into a room full of wooden desks, all mostly identical.

'Hey there,' said a figure in grey clothes. 'Why are you two in such a rush?' He was working at a huge filing cabinet, surrounded by stacks of papers almost as tall as the children, which half blocked their exit.

Valentine and Philomena didn't dare slow down. They darted between the piles, but with not quite enough space to squeeze through, knocked the biggest one over. Thousands of loose letters and sheets of paper scattered over the floor as the figure cried out in dismay.

Valentine and Philomena dodged past him, shouting apologies as they went.

The Never was there, crashing and banging its way

towards them. It was so cold now that Valentine's breath billowed into hot clouds as he ran.

'This is hopeless,' Philomena panted. 'There's nowhere to go. Maybe we should give up.'

'Never,' said Valentine.

'Do you trust him?'

'Who?'

'Death.' She leaned against the wall for three seconds' worth of deep breaths, then pushed back off and carried on running.

'I think so.' He had trusted him entirely, but Philomena's doubts were creeping into his mind, too. What if Death was just hiding somewhere, waiting for the Never to fix his problems? But it was too late now.

They turned a corner, no longer thinking about which fork to take, just moving. Valentine ran head first into something black and he shrieked, certain for a second that the Never had beaten them, found some other way through and cut them off. He put both arms across his face as a shield.

'There you are!' said Death. 'I was so worried about you!'

Valentine laughed with shaky relief.

'How did you get this far without being noticed?'

Behind Death, another figure in black was approaching – another figure with the hooded cape. Another reaper.

'All right,' said Death, 'stay calm.'

The reaper approached from one direction, as the Never

approached from the other. Finally the reaper lowered its hood.

'How do.' It was Mother Mercy.

'How did *you* get in here?!' said Death.

'Got the cloak from the librarians. Anything the souls ask for, they'll get.'

'But you're not—' Death began.

'But how did you get here before us?' Valentine interrupted.

'You took the long way round,' she said, 'and I had some help.' She swished aside the front of her cloak to reveal Captain Bones in her arms. 'Not a bad little tracking dog, after all.'

Bones was delighted to see them. She put him down and he jumped up at Valentine's legs

'Um, Valentine,' said Philomena, 'you're forgetting . . .' She took hold of his hand once again and suddenly the Never was there. It had crept closer while they weren't touching – he hadn't seen it filling up the end of the corridor until there was only a void where the walls should be.

'What is it?' said Mercy, peering the same way.

Death offered her his hand. 'I'll show you.'

'Ooof,' said Mercy. 'That's a nasty thing and no mistake.'

And then, as if the Never had noticed Mercy for the first time, it seemed to draw back a little.

'Did you see—?'

'It can't be . . . It's frightened of her!' marvelled Valentine.

'And well it might be!' said Mercy. She rolled up her sleeves and stepped towards it, and sure enough, it recoiled from her. 'Ahhhh, you know what I am, then? You can sense it, can you? I'm not like the others. You try it, and I'll give you what-for!'

'She's not going to punch the Never, is she?' said Valentine.

'Get going,' said Death. 'She won't hold it off for ever. It'll get past her or find some other way through.'

'But which way do we go?' said Philomena.

'Go with them,' said Mercy. 'I'll hold things down here.'

'You won't be able to see it once I let go,' warned Death.

'I don't need to see it to show it who's boss.' She shook a fist at the Never.

Death let go of her hand. 'This way. I hate this place,' he said. 'Gives me the heebie-jeebies.'

'I can see the people here,' said Philomena, peeping through a slightly open door, 'without holding on to Valentine.'

'That's because they're not strictly people. Not human people anyway,' said Death. 'But we must not let them see you. We've scouted out the quietest route with the least chance of getting caught. Then we'll have to hope Mercy holds the Never back long enough for you two to plead your case to the Higher-Ups.'

'And what's our case?' said Philomena.

'I don't know,' said Death. 'But if it's not convincing, you two will go into the Never and I'll end up fishing dead rats out of the River Thames. So think of something good.'

'What?' said Valentine. 'That's the whole plan?'

'I didn't say it was a good plan.' He stopped at a door that was slightly ajar. He nudged it a little further open.

Death put his head through the gap in the door and looked around.

'The coast is clear; we're nearly there.' He tiptoed out into the room, beckoning them to follow. 'This used to be Linda's office. You can tell by the frosty atmosphere.'

They crossed the room behind him, walking as softly as they could. They passed a desk with a little triangular name plate on it that read Linda and a small, spiky potted plant.

'Oh, I know,' quipped Death. 'Say the paperwork was done wrong by Linda, and you were supposed to have another forty years. Might as well bring her down with us, eh?'

'Hey,' came a voice from behind them.

All three turned sharply. There was a black cloak. A face covered by a hood. A reaper – no, three reapers were coming through the doorway into the little office.

'You're not supposed to be in this area,' said one of them.

'Ah . . .' said Death. 'I can explain. I'm on an errand, you see—'

'Who are they?' said another.

'Is that a mortal?' added the third.

'Ha!' squeaked Death. 'Imagine that! Who would ever bring a mortal here!'

'Two mortals,' the first corrected. 'Get them.'

Valentine and Philomena jumped back as the reapers advanced on them.

'New plan, Valentine,' said Death, pulling his watch out of his cloak and opening it. 'Run.'

Death hurled his watch down on to the floor with the crunch of broken glass. Golden dust exploded from it, not only on to the ground but also shooting upwards in dazzling streams. It filled the air in an instant, a glittering smoke cloud billowing up between the children and the reapers.

'Run!' Death shouted.

They ran.

The Inevitable Conclusion

Valentine and Philomena ran up the next corridor as fast as their feet would go. Ahead of them was a junction, a crossroads in the hallway with three directions to choose from. How would they ever find the right way without Death?

At that moment there was a fluttering and something flew over them, wings almost brushing their heads.

'Atropos!' Valentine gasped with relief. The bird didn't stop or look back at them as she swooped along the corridor and turned hard right up ahead.

'That way,' panted Philomena. At the turning point she glanced back.

'Is it here?' said Valentine.

'Not yet,' said Philomena. 'But I can feel it. Mother Mercy

is holding it off for now, but it's getting stronger.'

Atropos was waiting on the floor. She took off again. The corridor met another at right angles at the end, and she flew to the left. The children scrabbled along behind her, struggling to keep up.

'What was that?' came a voice from out of sight.

Valentine and Philomena halted, pressing themselves flat against the wall and holding their breath.

'What?' said another voice. Two figures passed the opening at the end of the corridor, emerging from where Atropos had flown.

'I could swear I saw a bird or something,' said the first.

'Weird,' said the other. They continued on without spotting Valentine and Philomena, who peeled away from the wall with relief.

The figures were disappearing round another bend in the corridor by the time Valentine reached it.

'We're safe,' he whispered to Philomena.

There was only one direction they could go once they reached the next turn in the path, and Atropos was waiting for them at the furthest end.

Philomena grabbed Valentine's wrist. 'Windows.'

All along this corridor were doors, each with large glass panes that would give any occupants a clear view of anyone walking past.

They stuck close to the sides, scurrying up to the first door, then ducking down to shuffle past the window. Up again, running a few steps, then duck and shuffle. It was taking for ever, and that was more time than they had. Valentine wasn't sure if they were quiet enough, because the pounding of his heart and his anxious breathing were deafening.

It came with great relief when they reached the last of the doors without incident, and Atropos headed off again, showing them the way. The next two corridors were in near darkness, and they could barely make out the sheen of Atropos's feathers as she led them deeper and deeper into this labyrinth.

'How much further?' said Valentine, although he knew the crow couldn't answer. His legs were already aching.

'I can hear the rumbling,' said Philomena. 'It's getting nearer.'

Atropos led them to a doorway and the other side was so brightly lit that Valentine had to shade his eyes until they adjusted to the change. They found themselves halfway up a huge staircase, spiralling for at least ten floors in each direction.

'Oh no,' said Valentine as Atropos took off, flying up through the centre and right towards the top.

'Oh no,' said Philomena, but she was looking down instead, staring over the railings into the long drop below.

Valentine came to her side and put his hand on her shoulder, peering down to see what she saw.

The Never. It was down there and slowly rising, a terrible black tide, swallowing stair after stair, thin tendrils reaching upwards.

Running again, they climbed and climbed and climbed. Philomena kept glancing down to check how close the Never was. Valentine, a few steps ahead, wished he could see it too. It didn't matter. They only thing they could do was keep going.

And finally, they were at the top. Corridors stretched off from the landing, and directly in front of them were three steps up to a grand oak door with the number thirteen in large brass letters. Atropos waited on the top step.

'Is this it?' panted Valentine. 'The Higher-Ups?'

Atropos cawed and bowed a yes.

'We made it.' His whole body, his heart, his soul was trembling. His entire universe rested on the next moments, and whoever was behind that door. 'We just need to make our case and then . . .'

'I can't,' said Philomena.

Valentine took her hand to reassure her, then instantly realized what she meant. The Never was very close now. He could hear it swallowing up the air, and taste the chill of the void. It was four floors below them, and still steadily rising. If they went into that chamber, they would have to stop running for long enough to explain themselves. The Never would swallow Philomena up before they'd even had chance to ask for help.

'Keep running!' said Valentine. 'I'll go in alone. If you keep moving—'

She nodded, gasping for breath. Valentine knew she was already exhausted – he hoped her strength would last. His heart was almost wrenched from his chest as she disappeared from view. If he didn't fix things, he'd never see her again.

'Atropos – go with her, show her the best way.'

In response, the bird clucked and ruffled her feathers, then turned her head and dipped her beak. With a sharp tug, she plucked the one white feather from her tail, and as she took off, dropped it from her beak. It drifted down towards Valentine.

He didn't know why she did it, but she must have had a reason. He snatched the feather from the air, shoved it into his pocket, and charged through the doorway.

The chamber beyond was not unlike the bursar's office at the Foundling Hospital.

Wood-panelled walls. Richly patterned rugs. A tall desk, and behind it, head bowed low over a stack of papers . . .

'Yes?'

Linda.

Valentine gasped.

Linda hated Death, and she hated rule-breaking. What hope did he have of convincing her? She'd throw him out the moment she set eyes on him.

'What do you want?' Linda peered down at Valentine disdainfully.

Of course. She didn't recognize him. Valentine had seen Linda, but she had never seen him, and she had no idea that he was Death's illegal apprentice. He forced the muscles in his face to relax and hide his surprise. This didn't change anything. He simply needed to make his argument in Philomena's favour. Except, now that he was actually here, he didn't know what to say or where to begin.

Valentine took a deep breath. 'I need help. I need to make a change to this book.' He produced Philomena's book from his pocket and placed it on the desk 'I need to give her more life. I need the Permanent Ink. Quickly. Please.'

'Why?' Linda picked up the book between two fingers and wrinkled her nose, as though it were dirty.

'She missed her death time, and the Never is after her, right now.' Would the ink be locked in a cupboard somewhere? Behind one of the doors leading on? He hoped it wasn't in a different place entirely. He was sure Philomena couldn't keep the Never at bay for more than a minute or two longer.

'As it should be,' said Linda, idly flicking through the pages with very little interest. 'That's what the Never is for.'

'But it's not her fault. Please. If we extend her life even a little bit . . .'

'Young man,' said Linda in a tone so sharp it might as well have been an insult, 'every human wants their life extended. Rules are rules. They die when they're supposed to.'

'Can't you make an exception?' Valentine pleaded.

'I take the rules very seriously. How do you think I got promoted to level thirteen?'

'By following the rules?'

'By following the rules! No exceptions. Not for saints or heroes or anyone. Why is this a special case?'

'I—' His brain was whirling and sparking and struggling for the right answer.

Linda closed the book and pushed it back towards Valentine. 'She's just an ordinary person. Not important at all.'

'She's important to me!' Valentine wondered where Philomena was, if she was still running, if he would be able to tell when the Never swallowed her. 'She's my kindred spirit.'

'Ha,' said Linda, humourlessly, eyes already back on her work. 'Ridiculous. Reapers don't have kindred spirits; that's a mortal thing.'

'But—' He stopped himself before he could say *I am mortal.* If Linda found out that Death had taken a human apprentice, he and Death would be in danger, too.

'I can't even consider the case unless you have evidence that somehow this girl is different from the millions of others—'

'No!' Valentine made his choice. 'But I'm different.'

He rummaged through the vast pockets of his cloak until he found the tatty folded paper right at the bottom. He opened it up and slammed it down on the table. Linda sat back and blinked indignantly.

'Look.' Valentine jabbed the page. 'I'm mortal, and I was apprenticed to Death for seven years.'

She spluttered. 'What is this?' Snatching up the paper, she squinted furiously at it, then at Valentine, then back to the paper.

'It's evidence. Apprenticeship papers. I'm mortal, but I have to spend seven years collecting souls and living away from humans and being a reaper.'

'That's not possible! You can't be. The rules of the universe say no human apprentices.'

'But I am,' Valentine insisted. 'This is proof. And the rules of apprenticeship say I *must* be a reaper for seven years. This place –' he gestured all round him – 'has taken seven mortal years from me. That's why this case is different. Because you owe me seven years. And I want you to give them to her.'

Valentine put his hand on Philomena's book and looked Linda straight in the eye. And waited.

All of eternity ticked by, his words lingering in the air like smoke, his heart thudding and thumping. He felt terrified. And he felt powerful.

The papers were trembling in Linda's hand. Her lips pressed together in a thin, furious line and her eyebrows squeezed together in confusion.

'I don't . . .' she muttered. 'This can't . . . A human . . . But the rules . . .'

She pulled an enormous book from a shelf behind her and laid it out on the desk with a thud, licking her finger and leafing hurriedly through the pages.

'I don't know what the rule is. There is no rule in the book for this. It's never happened before.'

'You're level thirteen,' said Valentine. 'The highest there is. Make a new rule.'

Linda froze. She turned her head towards Valentine and frowned, suspiciously, and then gradually, the frown faded into a gleeful half-smile. 'A new rule,' she repeated, quietly. 'I say, that would be something, wouldn't it? Adding a whole new rule to the book . . .'

She returned to flipping pages with a new purpose. 'The rules do say that a new rule can be added . . .' She traced the rows of writing, then tapped a particular spot. '*In exceptional circumstances.* I never thought I'd have the chance . . .'

Valentine was sure his heart would escape from his chest if it beat any harder.

'Please,' said Valentine. 'She's running out of time.'

Linda nodded. 'I accept your request.'

Valentine almost fainted on the spot, but he had to hold himself together for a minute longer.

'There will have to be a full investigation, of course—'

'Yes, fine, where's the ink?!' Valentine snatched up Philomena's book. There wasn't time for any more talking. What if it was already too late, and the Never had eaten her while they were arguing?

'Through there.' Linda pointed towards a doorway covered over with a curtain. Valentine was through it in half a second.

There it was. Permanent Ink. The answer to everything, just sitting there, in a little glass bottle on a table in an empty room.

Valentine put the book down, open to the last page, and prised the stopper out of the bottle of ink.

Pen. There was no pen.

He looked all around, lifted the book, checked on the floor – there was no pen.

Darting back to the curtain, he yanked it out of the way and shouted to Linda. 'I need a pen, quickly!'

289

'There isn't one.'

'What?!'

'You're supposed to have your own. That's the rule. Use a quill from your wings.'

'I don't have wings!' said Valentine. 'I'm human.'

'What a pity,' said Linda.

Then he remembered. Atropos. That clever bird. It was still there, in his pocket, the white feather from her tail. He dipped it into the ink and crossed out the last line of the book with shaky hands. The ink settled comfortably into the paper. Permanent.

There was only a tiny gap for him to write in. He hesitated for a moment and then wrote:

In the Sweet Hereafter

There should be bells ringing, or angels singing, or *something*, surely? Had it even worked?

'Is she safe?' Valentine ran back through the curtain, clutching Philomena's book in both hands. 'Has the Never stopped?'

'The Never can't stop,' said Linda. 'Because it never existed in the first place. But if you mean has it stopped trying to eat her soul, then yes.' She pulled on a velvet rope hanging beside her chair, and a figure appeared at one of the doorways.

'Amazing news, Gary. I'm adding a new rule to the book!' said Linda, clapping her hands together. She glanced at Valentine, then seemed to catch herself and returned to her usual serious demeanour. 'Oh, and have somebody find the girl,' she said. 'And Death. Bring them here.'

The figure nodded and then retreated.

'What happens next?' said Valentine. Relief washed over him, but there was still trouble in the air. Linda knew about him now, and about Death's rule-breaking.

Before Linda could answer, the main door swung open and Philomena stumbled in, Atropos right behind her. She threw her arms round Valentine.

'It's gone,' she said. 'It had me cornered, Valentine. It started to twist round me, and I closed my eyes and then –' she shivered violently – 'then all of a sudden the whole world came back. It was like waking up from a nightmare.'

'I'm so glad you're safe.'

The bird came to rest on Linda's desk and gave a neat little bow of greeting.

'And you, Atropos,' said Valentine. 'Thank you.' He tentatively reached out to her, and for the first time she allowed him to stroke her soft wings.

'Ahem,' said Linda.

They all turned their attention back to her.

'Young lady,' she began. 'I have been made aware of a unique situation, and as such, I have decided to extend your life, for the duration of . . .' She frowned and waved towards Valentine. 'Name, mortal?'

'Oh, Valentine, miss. Valentine Crow.'

'For the duration of Valentine Crow's apprenticeship. While he is acting as a reaper, his mortal years will be allocated to you.'

'I'll be a reaper for ever, then,' said Valentine. Philomena hugged him again.

'That is not part of the agreement,' said Linda, sternly. 'The indenture is for seven years. We will review this case then. I make no promises beyond that.'

'Thank you,' said Philomena. 'Thank you, thank you, thank you.'

Seven years. When he had first been claimed as Death's apprentice, seven years had felt like an eternity. Now it sounded like no time at all. Still, seven years was better than nothing.

Seven years was surely long enough to build a case for Philomena to stay longer.

'And I'm safe, too, right?' said Valentine, suddenly remembering what he'd risked to make this happen. 'You're not going to feed me to the Never?'

'Why would I do that?' said Linda.

'Because mortals aren't supposed to be reapers.'

'They certainly are not. But it appears you have the correct paperwork. We take that very seriously here.'

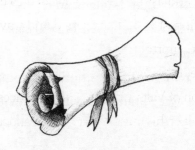

'So that means . . .' Valentine was thinking on his feet. He had betrayed Death, in a way, to save Philomena, because now the Higher-Ups knew about his illegal human apprentice. But Valentine had already solved one impossible problem that day, so he could solve this one, too. 'That means Death has to keep his job, too!'

'Death is in enormous trouble. This entire mess comes down to him meddling and bending the rules all over again. There will be consequences.'

'But I'm apprenticed to him. To learn his job. For seven years.'

Philomena caught on and jumped in to support him. 'And if Death's gone, that breaks the indenture. Which you take very seriously here.'

Linda put her hands on her hips and narrowed her eyes. She didn't have the towering height of Death, but she was plenty intimidating. 'Two mortal children dare to tell an eternal being how to run the afterlife?'

Atropos hopped from her perch and settled herself on Valentine's shoulders, the three of them in a line of solidarity.

'Death always said that humans were fascinating little creatures. I never really saw the appeal. But you make a fair point.'

'So . . .' Valentine urged.

'So he will remain in position to complete your apprenticeship as agreed, and we will also review his case in seven years.'

Valentine beamed. A win for all of them, then. Or at least, a reprieve. 'He won't be scraping dead cats out of gutters?'

'Oh, he'll absolutely be doing that, too. On top of his regular job. We can't let something like this go unpunished. It sets a bad precedent.' A glint in Linda's eyes suggested that she was looking forward to the punishment part. She crossed over to the door and held it open for them. 'But I'll deal with him later. Right now you need to get that book back to the library, and this mortal back to the land of the living.'

Honour'd Dust

Atropos guided them back the way they came, a more pleasant journey now they didn't need to run and hide. Though they peered warily round corners and down stairwells, there was no trace of the Never. It was as though it had never been there at all.

Which is true, in a way, thought Valentine, then pushed the idea from his head. He didn't want to ponder it for another second.

'Did you do it?' Death came bounding out from a side branch of the corridor.

'We did it,' said Valentine.

'I knew you would,' said Death. 'Clever humans with your clever little squishy wet brains.' He reached out two bony hands and ruffled both children's hair at the same time. 'Let's get out of here, then. This is no place for the living.'

Living. Philomena was living again. Success. Valentine handed her the book and she tucked it under her arm.

'Aren't you going to read what I wrote?'

She shook her head. 'We're not supposed to know what our book says, are we?' said Philomena. 'I'll do it properly. Wait until it's my time.'

Her time. Valentine discreetly opened the pocket watch – Philomena's hand was gone.

They turned a corner and there was Mercy, right where they had left her, still snarling and shouting insults up at where the Never had been. Captain Bones was still with her, fast asleep at her feet.

'It's gone now, you daft old bat. You can stop.' Death put his arm round her shoulder and tapped his bare teeth to the top of her head in a bony kiss. 'But thank you.'

'Don't be going all soft on me now, you mouldering bag of bones.'

Captain Bones's ears twitched at this. He woke and stretched, then noticed Valentine and stopped mid-yawn to race over and jump around him in excited circles.

'It's not too late, Mercy,' said Death. 'While we're down here. I'm sure the Higher-Ups would be happy to release you so you can finally go back to the Always.'

'Pah,' said Mercy and folded her arms across her chest. 'Nice try. Release me, indeed! I'm going nowhere.'

'Still as stubborn as ever,' said Death.

'And you've brought my apprentice back. About time too.' Mercy marched up to Philomena and inspected her closely, the same way she'd inspected Valentine on their first meeting. 'Not too badly damaged by the experience. A little bit of decomposition, but nothing we can't fix.' She turned and began heading towards the library.

Philomena pulled Valentine in for another hug. She felt warm. The world felt warm, too. 'Thank you, Valentine.'

'Come on!' shouted Mother Mercy. 'The likes of me and thee shouldn't be in a place like this.'

'You'll visit, won't you?' said Philomena, letting go. 'Lots and lots?'

'Promise,' said Valentine.

'Don't forget to give that book back to the librarians,' Death called after them.

'Linda knows about me now,' said Valentine. 'The illegal apprenticeship. I had to tell her.'

Death shrugged and nodded. 'That's all right. I knew as soon as we headed down here that the game was up.' He put his hand on Valentine's shoulder as they trudged back towards the waiting world.

'But you brought us here anyway.'

'You taught me something,' said Death. 'I'd forgotten, over the years, all the things that make mortals wonderful. Even though you're small and insignificant and your lifetimes are so short. You're basically bugs in clothes.'

'Rude,' said Valentine.

'Since the whole Mercy situation, I stopped taking much interest in human lives. They're just the gaps between deaths to me. But having you around reminded me how special and interesting you are.' He sighed. 'Not that it matters now. I'll hardly see a human now that I'm demoted.'

'Oh, about that—' They entered the library, peaceful and calm and quiet as if nothing had happened at all.

'I have to fly, Valentine,' said Death. 'We'll talk about everything later. Need to get this watch repaired before we end up with a whole bunch of missed death times. There's a good watchmaker on Partridge Street, I hear. Mister Dearth, or something.'

With that, Death pulled up his hood and with a swish of fabric, he was gone.

Valentine slowly made his way up the stairs to the mausoleum on weary legs. At least Death had left the slab open for him this time. He wandered out into the daylight and marvelled at the specks of golden dust that coated his clothes. Finally he lay down on the grass to rest.

For a moment, anyway. A buzzing from his pocket reminded him to check his watch.

Collection time.

THE
END

ABOUT THE AUTHOR

Jenni Spangler writes children's books
with a magical twist, she loves to take
real and familiar places and events and
add a layer of mystery and hocus-pocus.
She had the good fortune to be
selected for the first year of the
'Write Mentor' scheme and was
mentored by Lindsay Galvin,
author of *The Secret Deep*.
Jenni lives in Staffordshire with
her husband and two children.
She loves old photographs,
picture books and tea,
but is wary of manhole covers
following an unfortunate incident.

Read on for an extract from another magical
Jenni Spangler book:

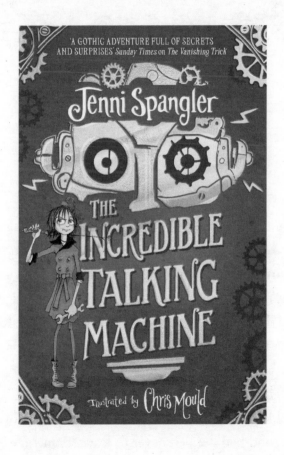

'A GOTHIC ADVENTURE FULL OF SECRETS
AND SURPRISES' *Sunday Times* on *The Vanishing Trick*

Jenni Spangler

THE INCREDIBLE TALKING MACHINE

Illustrated by Chris Mould

Lights Up

All theatres are haunted.

Manchester's Theatre Royale was haunted by a dead opera singer known as Cold Annie. Actors complained of an icy, creeping dread whenever they used the dressing room that had once belonged to her, and stagehands avoided the places she was said to roam late at night. Rumour was that if she appeared before a performance, it was sure to go horribly wrong.

But Tig Rabbit wasn't scared.

She liked to imagine that Cold Annie simply loved the theatre, and had decided never to leave. Sometimes, when Tig was waiting alone in the dark to lift the curtains, or tidying the costumes away late at night, she had the sensation that Annie was nearby. It made her feel less lonely.

She'd mentioned this once to Gus, the carpenter's boy, who was two years older and considered himself superior. This was a mistake. Ever since, he'd teased her about how stupid it was to believe in ghosts. Still, Tig noticed he never went into Annie's dressing room, and he was nowhere to be found when it was time to go into the dark auditorium to light or extinguish the lamps.

That was why, even though Gus was supposed to do it an hour ago, Tig was lighting the lamps herself. The new act would be here any moment, and they'd all be in trouble if the job wasn't done. Typical of Gus, the coward, to shirk his duties. She'd get him back for it.

In the blackness at the edge of the stage, she set her foot on the bottom rung of a ladder which stretched up, taller than a house, into the rigging above. The auditorium was so quiet Tig could hear the flicker of the tiny flame at the end of her long lamp-lighting stick. There were no windows in the cavernous room so although it was early afternoon dark stillness wrapped around her like a blanket, pushing against the feeble light.

Tig didn't mind. She could do this with her eyes closed. Carefully she climbed, one hand clutching the light-stick and the other keeping her balance on the rungs. Thirty-two steps to the flies, where long beams spanning the width of the stage held a complicated web of ropes and pulleys. Dizzyingly high, hidden from the sight of the audience – this was Tig's world.

Some days she felt like a ghost herself, inhabiting the secret in-between spaces of the Royale. She walked through the walls, crouched behind the scenery, crawled beneath the seats. If needed, she could travel from basement to roof without being seen by a single living soul. It made her feel like she belonged, that she was a small part of the theatre magic – that she was home. A home full of long hours and hard work and a frustrating boss, a home very different to the one she had lived in before her father died, but a home all the same.

Reaching the top of the ladder, she pulled herself up onto a narrow walkway, holding the light-stick ahead of her as she found her footing.

The stage lights were the pride of the Royale. New-fangled gas lamps – the first theatre in Manchester to install them. They were brighter, and far easier, than lighting the place with candles, but there was a knack to it. There were two rows of five lamps – one at each side of the stage. Tig leaned over the edge of the walkway and used the clover-shaped hook on the end of the light-stick to twist the valve, allowing gas to flow down the long, shiny pipes and ooze out of each lamp.

Now she had to be fast. She touched the flame of the

light-stick to the top of the first lamp and with a pop and a flare of heat it burst into life. She ran to the next light. Pop. Two flames lit.

Every wasted second let gas seep into the air, the eggy sulphur smell warning Tig to act quickly. If too much gas escaped it might cause an explosion, and the whole theatre would go up in smoke. She ran along the line, her footsteps on the metal walkway echoing off the high ceiling, pausing briefly to light each lamp in turn.

One side done. Already the theatre was transformed. Warm, yellowish light washed over the stage and painted Tig's shadow as a giant on the wall behind her. The glow spilled out beyond the edge of the stage, catching the golden scrolls and vines that decorated the royal boxes and illuminating the first few rows of empty seats.